Cupid

is a

S. S. Nightshade

ISBN: 979-8-9936685-1-2

Nightshade's Writing Desk LLC

For the college kids surviving off

of iced coffee and spite

This story, though heartfelt and humorous, includes representations of **mental health** and the **recovery from an abusive relationship**. As such it is intended for readers 18+

As those themes are present, there may be moments that are triggering to some readers. Topics include but are not limited to:

~ Panic attacks

~ Severe anxiety disorder

~ Illusions of depression and PTSD

~ Sudden bursts of anger

~ Cupids Bow spurs the reference of active shooter drills on school grounds, though no threat is posed or described

~ **In the context of the previously abusive relationship:**

sexual coercion and abuse, emotional abuse and manipulation, abuse of power

Chapter 1

My best friend was doing body shots with Cupid and didn't even know it. I could barely form a coherent thought over the drum of the bass behind me, but I could see perfectly fine. And his mouth was all over her damn abdomen. Pervert.

I had the unfortunate experience of figuring out who the hell he was by calling 911 on his ass. Somehow, I was the only person in the whole quad who saw this guy squatting on top of the language arts building with a crossbow. When the paramedics arrived, *I* was the one shipped off to the hospital for a psych eval and tox screen since there was no video footage of him going up there and he had no weapons on him or in his dorm room.

A room my dumbass stormed into when I was finally released.

Cupid—Carter—was a junior social sciences major, and a member of our school's notorious frat house Heavens Boys. Yes, they literally call themselves that.

He didn't even flinch when I stormed in, spewing incoherent accusations while videotaping on my cell in case he pulled another weapon out of nowhere. The calm grin on his face was somehow more unnerving than any violent thing he could have done. And that's what I blame for freezing.

When I was finally done yelling, literally panting from my fit in his doorway, he took me by surprise. The door was suddenly slammed shut, my wrists pinned above my head, and his tongue slid into my mouth before I could even move. And of course, my phone kept on dutifully recording, capturing every shocked and needy sound that left me from just a stupid kiss.

A kiss that cleared my head of my anger long enough to hear the few words he offered. He was a fifteenth generation Cupid. He didn't know how I could see him while he worked. He promised not to scare me again.

And then the bastard opened the door and waltzed downstairs like nothing happened.

That was a week ago, but the rest of Heavens Boys still hadn't let it go. That's why I was here, DJing this party for free with all my tech at risk of being destroyed by the elements. And if not by the elements, the drunk underclassmen.

Why they were having a back-to-school party outside in January in New

England was beyond me. Sure, the school had sprung for a few of those fancy stand up heaters for the house, but it was still ridiculous. Add in all these drunk assholes spilling their drinks everywhere, it was a damn miracle my shit wasn't broken already.

More than once, I had to drag people off the makeshift stage in the corner of the backyard. Every two minutes I was shoving half-filled solo cups off my equipment, uncaring of the wasted alcohol and ignoring the complaints from their owners. My sound system was worth more than a grand, then add in my speakers and tech? Yea, they could get a fresh drink, fuck em.

So here I sat, atop my oldest subwoofer which I lugged around for nostalgias sake, watching a bunch of wasted frat and sorority kids shriek out the lyrics to Sweet Caroline like possessed chihuahuas.

Carter had been lingering around since early this afternoon when I arrived to set up. He probably thought he was gallant by offering to give me a tour of the house, which obviously I declined. Then offered to help me set up, which I forcefully declined. Then sat around anyway, yapping about his family in Chicago, what girls were expected to come tonight and other stupid crap I didn't care about.

Seriously, the guy was like a walking talking golden retriever, seeking out my attention and showing off until his frat brothers finally dragged him away giving me some semblance of peace. I really couldn't tell if he was trying to make up for my panicked first impression of him, or if he was trying to get back at me for it. Honestly, I wouldn't blame him if he was. I knew what being wrongfully detained felt like.

So, I had been ignoring him as best as I could for the six hours I've been stuck here—but his tongue was now on Jennys belly. Lapping up the alcohol which had slipped down over her hips, making her squeal and laugh. I knew exactly what that tongue felt like.

"Yo DJ! Play something with spirit!" A chorus of roars went up at my expense as I stood, approaching my soundboard. I tugged my gloves off with my teeth and slid my headphones back on, drowning their cries out.

At least like this I could pretend I was actually doing what I loved *where* I preferred. Two nights a week I worked at a club in downtown Providence. Not my dream job, but the best I could get without an internship. And after I received my masters, maybe I could finally get out of here and land a gig in LA. Find some independent artists, produce some music with them, and earn enough to open my own label.

With that in mind, I put some effort back into what I was doing. Though I didn't care for the setting, this was still technically practice and experience that I could tuck into my portfolio. And the more energy I put into it the warmer I got, so it wasn't a total waste even if it was for these pricks.

It was easy to tune them out and find my rhythm, head nodding along to the beat as it rose, blended. Trap merging seamlessly with techno, the lyrics from one of those girly pop songs from the early 2010's scattered out as it rose, rose, rose... drop.

The grin that curved my mouth was genuine when they all started going nuts. This is what I liked. Controlling a crowd. Making them have a full body experience.

Alcohol or not, music was magic, and it did that for everyone if it was wielded right.

"Jackie Jackie Jackie!" Jenny clambered up next to me, slinking her arms around my waist from behind. She was the only one allowed up here and knew how protective I was of my gear, so she always kept my body between her and it.

"You drunk?" I asked, shifting my headphones off of one ear so I could hear her better. She giggled and held up a hand, mimicking a pinch.

"Little bit." I grunted, resisting the urge to roll my eyes. At least her coat was back on. Like she could read my thoughts, she laughed and added, "I'm perfectly fine, so stop jumping to every horrible conclusion. You should also let loose a bit, relieve some stress."

"Stop evaluating me, doctor."

Unlike me, Jenny was going to get a job which would actually make her money once she graduated. She was a few years younger than me, just starting her first year of master's in child psychology.

When we met as undergrads, I had no idea what the hell she wanted from me. She was so bubbly and friendly I was half afraid she wanted to date. Apparently, I wasn't subtle about swinging the other way though. Her presence and support were actually a really big part of me continuing my master's degree here rather than fleeing after what happened in my senior year of undergrad.

"Soooo," she drawled, plucking a solo cup off one of my speakers before I could curse the kid out and do it myself. Damn freshman. "How are we feeling being around Carter?"

I hesitated slightly, the bolt of anxiety coursing through me shaking off my rhythm. Jenny didn't know about what happened in Carter's room, nobody did. As far as anyone here was concerned, tonight was the first time I had to see and interact with him since I almost got him arrested.

"I'm fine," I finally grumble out, hands flying over the soundboard as I started shifting the beat to something faster. Harder. Pounded my anger out through the music like I'd taught myself to do. "Though I almost gagged watching him lick you like a dog."

She tilted her head back, laughing in that gorgeous way of hers. Jenny never had any issues attracting attention, and she thrived in it to boot. Like a star, her warm glow just made everyone gravitate towards her.

"He was a gentleman about it." I scoffed. No way in hell I was going to believe that after his little stunt with me. And as if summoned...

Carter plucked a cup out of a kid's hand who was just about to set it down next to the extension cord that half of my wires were plugged into. I felt Jenny perk up behind me, which just made me bristle further. No way in hell was I letting her—

"Can I request a song, Jackson?" Carters million-watt smile did nothing to ease the immediate flair of annoyance which made my skin tingle. Everyone called me Jackie. Even the professors by now since I've been here for damn near eight years, and almost all of them had an idea of what had happened.

"No," I said flatly, switching out one of my tapes, and purposefully making the music louder to drown him out.

"Jackie!" Jenny hissed in my ear, elbowing me lightly. "Don't be rude. You even let the freshman request!" I shot her a look of betrayal, but Carter just kept grinning, those dark eyes of his studying me with hidden calculation.

It wasn't like I was scared of him after what he did. The physicality of it was a shock, but my issue lies with what he *was*, not what he did to me.

In the past week I had grown nothing short of obsessed after his outlandish claims, hitting the library every night and neglecting my own work to study up on what a Cupid was. Turns out, it's not the capitalist profit image of a half-naked cherub with an oversized bow made of clouds shooting people at random with heart tipped arrows.

This guy claims to somehow be connected to one of the original Greek

Gods, Eros. The earliest information I could find on him was dated before 1000BC, and the love web of his role was complicated to say the least.

Jenny pinched my elbow again, drawing me back to the present. The dubstep clashing in my head was a stark contrast against Carters curly blonde hair and pleading doe eyes. Christ.

"Please?" He whined and I could barely mask my disgust. Of course he would be drunk and whining. I heaved a sigh, flexing my cold fingers. If I gave him what he wanted maybe he would scram. Then I could run a disc for a while and put my gloves back on.

"Fine," I grumbled, shifting my gaze back to the soundboard. "One song."

"Hmm." In half a second he'd replaced Jenny at my back, making me freeze as he rested his chin on my shoulder. "How about, DJ Got Us falling In Love?"

I didn't even try to hold back the scoff which slipped past my lips. Ignoring his lingering weight at my back I already started adjusting the beat for the switch, free hand flying across the keyboard of my way too old laptop to pull up the audio.

"Can I try?" One of his hands had snaked between my raised arm and waist, fingers hovering over the switches. Heart racing, I snatched his hand midair, turning my head to glare at him.

"You'll break it."

"I'll be gentle." The slow smirk curving his lips told me he knew exactly where my mind went with that comment. I shrugged roughly, forcing him to lift his head off my shoulder and take half a step back. Seriously, what was his deal?

"Get off my stage Carter."

Sensing the mounting tension Jenny intervened, sliding between the pair of us and looping her arm through one of his. I both loved her for it yet felt my paranoia skyrocket.

"Carter why don't you come dance with me before your songs over?" She prompted, easing him off the stage with her. He kept his gaze locked on mine though, something burning there that I didn't want to address because there was only one clear thought in my head now.

If Cupid shot my best friend, I would fucking kill him.

Chapter 2

It's been two days since the party, but my anxiety continued to race. As far as I could tell, Carter hadn't done anything to Jenny. She wasn't goo goo eyed or gushing about him. Actually, she hadn't mentioned him at all. I'd kept my eye on them for the three songs they'd danced together before he'd let her slip away. Other than nursing a hangover the next morning, she was still my normal Jenny.

Despite my aversion to him, I found myself increasingly curious as to how it all worked. Obviously, the bow and arrow part carried over, though I hadn't actually seen him shoot one off. When I'd seen him up there, at first I was scared because I thought he was going to jump. Then when I made out the crossbow for what it was, I felt a whole different type of fear. One endorsed by a decade of active shooter drills.

But thinking back to it, he had just been standing there, staring through the scope. He was so busy people watching he didn't even notice me screaming at him at first. And then in his room he did say he didn't know how I could see him while he was working, like he did this all the time and never got caught.

For the fifth time I snapped the lead on my pencil, and I cursed under my breath. My notes were a damn mess because I wasn't paying attention, thoughts constantly circling back to Carter... Cupid.

I set my jaw, pushed the end of my led pencil slowly, easing out a fresh tip. After a beat I decided to write it, to get it out of my damn head.

Cupid.

"Hey Jackson."

My gaze whips up to find Carter standing opposite of me, our faces almost level since he's a step down. Then I'm turning my head back and forth, surprised to see the auditorium almost empty, the few lingering students almost packed up. Did I really just spiral through an hour-long lecture and not realize it?

"Sorry," he grins at me sheepishly, a hand running through his curls in a move that I'm sure got the girls to swoon. "I didn't mean to spook you. I just saw you through the window and wanted to chat."

His usual playfulness was replaced by a more serious undertone, his gaze flickering down to my notebook. "Unless you had work to—" I slam the book shut before he can make out what I've scribbled down, face flushing.

"...do," he finishes awkwardly, his brows pinching together in confusion.

"I have studio hours to complete." I don't but the excuse is believable enough for me to start haphazardly shoving my things into my bag. When I stand, he holds an arm out to block me.

"Can we walk and talk?" He asks, a bit more insistent than before.

"No." I'm already swinging my bag over my shoulder and untangling my old wire headphones. Carter plucks one from my fingers, putting it in his own ear before I can stop him and I feel my blush deepen.

Music had automatically started playing, but this wasn't hip music off the radio. It wasn't even any of the eccentric beats I made at work. We stood there in silence as my own voice filled our ears, a demo for an album I had given up on.

"What the hell is wrong with you?" I finally bite out, yanking the earbud away from him and slamming out the auditorium door. I didn't play my music for anyone, not since—

"Jackson we really do need to talk," he called after me, catching up easily with his longer legs. "About what happened in my room."

"Will you shut up?" I hiss, glancing nervously at the other students in the hall, but they were wholly ignoring us. So much so that I almost got run over if not for Carter grabbing me by the hood and yanking me back into his chest.

I could feel his heartbeat against my spine, rampant as mine was. He heaved a breath, releasing his hold on me but didn't step away.

"I told you. People can't usually see me when I work."

"Then how come I just almost got run over?" I retort, regaining some distance between us and he had the audacity to grin again.

"Because I marked you at the party." He taps the back of his neck. "When I was leaning on you making my song request. You didn't feel it?"

"Obviously not!" My voice rose to almost a yell but not a single person glanced at me. I turned on my heel, damn near sprinting for the bathroom. Leaning over the sink I craned my neck, lifting my hair off the back of my neck with one hand and using my phone's camera to figure out what the hell he meant.

A rose-tinted stain sat perfectly centered an inch under my hairline. A god damn kiss mark.

"Before you find something to throw at me," Carters voice echoed from the doorway, sounding overly self-satisfied. "I only did it to avoid SWAT being called for a second time. There's only so many criminal allegations I can dodge," he added with a chuckle. "Now while I'm working, no one can see or hear you. Except for me of course."

"So, you're working right now?" I growled out, finding him in the reflection and dropping my hair. Then pull up my hood for good measure. "What the hell does that entail?" He hums, sounding satisfied that I asked.

"See? You are interested."

"Carter."

"Alright alright." He holds his hands up in mock surrender. "I'll show you exactly how it's done. If you let me buy you a coffee first."

I glared at him through the glass, but he held it with a steady, warm gaze of his own. Manipulative little shit.

I tell myself I'm not surrendering as I avert my gaze. That I'm not losing whatever this battle between us is. I need to know what he's doing, for Jenny's sake at the very least. She's been my best friend for five years, so I know when she's into a guy. Now I could do my damned best to keep her away from Carter, but I couldn't protect her from his bow if I didn't understand how it worked.

Plus, free coffee. Any master's student would take that bribe.

Carter's grin is unwavering as I slide past him and back into the hall, turning towards the cafeteria. Then I nearly jump out of my skin as he slides his hand into mine.

"There's a better café across campus," he says, tugging me after him gently. I stare at our joined hands in a mix of embarrassment and outrage. Like he can feel the tension radiating off of me he glances back, softening slightly. "No one can see us, so you don't need to be embarrassed."

"That's not the—"

"Besides," he cuts me off, looking ahead again. "I'm just ensuring you don't run away from me is all."

My boiling emotions lower down to a simmer, still displeased, but relenting to his point. I was avoiding his charm like the plague and would continue to, but I needed information first. I wouldn't be able to calm down without it.

He holds my hand the entire way across campus, squeezing tighter every time I try to pull away. Even when I snap and start voicing my complaints, he remains unbothered, pulling me after him until I find myself settled in a corner booth of a café I'd never been in.

It was dark and quiet. Moody. Several students were clustered together in the other booths, an array of neon hair, fishnets, and art supplies. It irked me that he took me to a place I instantly liked.

"What would you like?" Carter asks, a knowing grin on his face and I huff.

"Something iced."

"Sweet?"

"Sure."

He finally ambles away, leaving me to stew in peace for a few minutes. I pull out my laptop while I wait, plugging my headphones into it and working out a few beats to steady my racing heart. Which instantly short circuits again when he slides into the booth next to me, leaning against me to watch what I'm doing.

"Does the concept of personal space not exist to you?" I snap, grabbing the coffee he had slid towards me and scooting away. His mouth is moving but I can't hear him with the music still in my ears, so I pause it, heaving a sigh.

"Can you repeat that?" I ask, forcing myself to sound calmer, taking a sip of the coffee to steady my nerves. Cold foam. Caramel. I liked it.

"The kiss," he repeats. "You returned it with enthusiasm, so I'm confused as to why you hate being near me now."

26

I choked, coffee spewing before he was even done. I was coughing so hard tears were brimming in my eyes, Carter startling next to me and holding a napkin to my face.

"I'm fine," I wheeze out, turning my enflamed face away from him. "Why the hell are you bringing that up now?"

"Well, I didn't Cupid you that day from the roof," he says, his hand rubbing soothing circles on my back. "So, I'm just trying to understand—"

"Forget it," I snapped again, and he actually flinched, like I'd hurt him. That just confused me even more. No, Jackson. Focus.

"How does it work?" I ask, less aggressively this time. "The bow. The... Cupid-ing?" He sat back, thumbs playing with the lid of his drink.

"You have me pegged as a manipulative, lustful maniac, don't you?" I was shocked into silence, and he just nodded his head once, keeping his gaze down.

"I came onto you pretty strong. I'm sorry about that." For the life of me he sounded genuine, but he went on.

"I'm not literally shooting people and making them fall in love. If you're familiar with the three fates and those lifelines they thread, I have limited access to them. When I see two people drifting closer, I can grasp those lines and the metaphorical shot functions as a gentle nudge towards a positive possibility. I can also do the opposite, pulling apart what might turn destructive."

"The shots not really metaphorical since I saw you with a crossbow," I grumble, not letting him skip over that point. He sips his drink, nodding like he'd forgotten that detail.

"Right. Every Cupid has its own method of grasping and maneuvering the lines. I'm a bit sentimental but have a taste for modern efficiency, so my tool as you saw is a crossbow." He furrows his brows, adding, "I still don't understand how you saw me though. When the magic is active, I revert to Eros's state. Normal mortals aren't supposed to be able to see me."

I steeple my hands in front of me, dropping my forehead against them. If I didn't just have a psych eval done, I would be tempted to go admit myself right now. Keeping my head down, I blow out a slow breath, focusing on the scent of coffee so I don't panic.

"You said you were working now," I grumble, staring hard at the table. "And that this mark makes me invisible when you work. That could be problematic."

I can't just turn invisible any time he has the call to intervene in someone else's love life. I'm almost done with my masters. I have work every freaking weekend. And LA...

"It'll fade over time, like a normal one." His voice is soft again, hand traveling north on my spine to settle at the base of my neck. Fingers threading through my hair in a way that has my breath catching against my will as he adds, "But I'm not going to let it until I figure out what to do with you."

I finally look over at him, but he's not teasing me like I thought he was. His fingers shift against my neck, pressing in on the mark he left on me. I surprise myself by shivering, and he tilts his head like it was fascinating.

"Those threads of fate. Those lines I can tug" he murmurs, leaning close enough I can feel his breath ghost across my lips. "I can't see yours."

Chapter 3

I flinch away from him as his hand cups my jaw. His eyes roam over me freely, pitching to a shade of brown so dark they border on black. He follows my retreat until I'm backed into the corner of the booth, caught between him, the seat and the table. His hand stays on me, the other pressed flat next to my head, refusing to budge even as I shove against him.

"What the hell do you mean you can't see my fate lines?" I ask, concern pitching my voice higher than I wanted. He seems to realize himself, leaning back slightly, but not as far as I want him to.

"It's just as unnerving for me," he says, reassurance coating the statement that doesn't stick.

"Like hell it is!" I snap, shifting enough to kick one of my legs up and into his ribcage. He barely moves from the impact, the hand beside me dropping to snatch my raised ankle. Then gives me one sharp tug forward, and we both freeze.

Honestly, I think we both stopped breathing for a second too. My legs are halfway around his waist now, his weight pushing forward and in, hovering over me.

"I just didn't want you to hurt yourself," he breaths out, voice rougher than before. That sets off all sorts of alarm bells in my head, and a concerning twist of butterflies that I wish I could ignore.

"Just... get off me before someone sees." I look away, swallowing hard, but the hand he has on my cheek coaxes me back.

"I told you. With my mark on you, they can't see or hear you when I'm working." That damn playful smile is on his face again, his thumb rolling across my lower lip in a way that's almost possessive.

"T-then get to work," I force out, jerking my chin out of his grip again as embarrassment floods me. If he keeps touching me like this I'm gonna—

"I'm working on you right now." He lets me keep my face turned but takes advantage of the gap I've left between my shoulder and neck, nuzzling me gently.

My head was already swimming, body fully alert of every millimeter we pressed against one another. I should shove him. Bust his damn lip. But the only coherent thought I could come up with was how he smelled like sugarcane.

That with everything else was confusing the hell out of me. Most other guys would be drenched in a musky or outdoor-like cologne, but Carter smelled like a damn candy shop, making me wonder what he tasted like.

Unaware of my tumultuous thoughts he pressed a soft kiss to my skin, chuckling when I jerked my head away. His voice was soft in my ear, gently asking, "Since I can't see your fate lines, will you teach me what you like so I can help you?"

"What do you—" I'm cut off by his tongue tracing my pulse point, a jolt rocking my whole body. "Carter... wait..."

"They can't see you," he whispers against my neck, then kisses the spot with more pressure this time. My eyes go half lidded against my will as he works his way down, shifting the collar of my jacket out of his way. When I flinch at the feel of his teeth he finally pulls back, searching my face.

"What?" I sound so freaking breathless I wish I'd just stayed quiet.

"Why are you scared?" I froze again, not expecting the question, my guard instantly going up.

"Other than a random ass guy pinning me in a booth and assaulting me?" I force myself to glare at him, but the bastard just smirks, eyes glittering.

"I'm not random. In fact, you know me quite well, better than most." He presses closer again, the hand holding my ankle inching up my calf. "And you haven't said to stop."

"Yes I did," I argue, eyes tracking his hand as it continues its slow perusal up my leg. He chuckles low, another kiss to my jaw.

"You said to wait. And I am."

"A freaking technicality!" He raises a brow at the outburst, his hand pausing on my thigh.

"Do you want me to stop?" His eyes are still dark pools, but his voice is steady. I don't know how I knew, but I didn't doubt for a second that if I said the words, he would stop immediately. So why couldn't I?

"Are you scared because I'm a man?" He asks gently, hand continuing its slow drag against me.

"What? No. That's not the issue here," I grumble out, averting my eyes again. I wasn't exactly trying to hide it, but it always seemed to surprise people when they found out I was gay.

"Then is it because no one's touched you like this before?" His hand curves over my hip, fingers brushing my ass but not pushing further.

"No," I grind out between grit teeth. "This situation is just so fucked up. This isn't normal. You're... I don't even know what the hell to call you at this point," I huff out, every ounce of self-control I have left focused on remaining as still as I can.

Carter actually laughs, the hand on my jaw shifting into my hair. Smoothing it back over my ear. Playing with the chain connecting my lobe to my cartilage.

"It's not unprecedented for a Cupid to share this type of experience with a human. It's not like we're doing anything wrong."

He must have felt the shift in me somehow, because after a beat of silence he leans away. Concern replaced the heat as I shifted back, sharply pulling my legs back to me.

His eyes don't leave me as I slip my laptop back in my bag, put my headphones on, and snatch what's left of my coffee. He even slides out of the booth when I lean into him roughly, an unspoken request to let me out.

"Don't touch me like that ever again," I mumble, refusing to make eye contact with him.

"Can I at least know what I did wro—"

"Everything!" His face fell and I instantly regretted it. I didn't know what to say, or how to explain myself. All I knew was I needed to get out of here, before everything I've rebuilt comes crumbling down.

"Just stay away from me and Jenny," I whisper, turning my back on him. Then blast my music so loud that I can't hear if he replies or not.

Chapter 4

Jenny was late but for once I didn't complain. I needed more time to mentally prepare before going to work, being surrounded by what used to be my version of heaven and now was just a paycheck.

If she noticed that I was more pent up than normal she didn't comment on it. She chattered away like normal from the passenger seat of my car, flipping through a stack of bubblegum pink flashcards.

"If you had a test, you could have called out," I mutter gruffly, slamming on the horn as another asshole cuts me off. She worked as a bottle girl at the same club I DJ at. I didn't like it, but despite the risks she seemed to enjoy the job. And I had to admit her tips were a hell of a lot better than mine.

"Next round of tuition is due in a month," she says with a sigh. "I want to have some money left over after that."

I pulled the car into the club's parking garage, beginning the process of unloading my gear. They had their own speakers and light systems, but I preferred my own equipment over their motherboard which had the tendency to glitch. The manager didn't give a shit so long as music kept playing and people kept dancing.

Once my soundboard, hard drives, and laptop were balanced on my cart, I started dragging it towards the elevator where Jenny was already waiting. She was always good about holding it for me, and kicking people out with kindness if I needed the space.

We part ways once we scan into the employee entrance, her darting back to the dressing rooms and me continuing my uphill path to the stage. I swear this was all the cardio I needed.

This stage though, was worth it. Hovering twenty feet over the dance floor and made completely from glass and steel, it felt like a throne more than a sound booth.

"Mornin' Jackie." Seth was already there, flipping buttons for soundcheck, but paused the second he saw the look on my face. "The hell happened to you?"

"Don't know what you're talking about, and it's almost eight at night," I murmur back, hauling the first of my drives off the cart and to my corner of the stage.

He and I dual spun here every Saturday and Sunday. I hated not having full control at first, but Seth was fast and creative, so it was easy to find a flow with him. And it was better to have another DJ up here if one of us needed a break rather than playing a tape till we got back.

"Don't pull that shit." He whacked me on the back of the head with a stack of flyers. "The last time you looked this mopey was after that freshman girl tried sucking face with you a month ago."

I grunted an uncommitted sound, focusing on my gear, and praying he would drop it. I wasn't so lucky.

"Is there someone's ass I need to kick?" He asked, shifting from amused to dead serious in seconds. I shook my head before he could jump off a cliff.

"Not like that, just... weird." Weird was an understatement. Cracked out. Insane. Unexpected, yet better than any of the other attention I'd gotten in years. Which made me hate it all the more.

"Weird," he echoed skeptically, plucking my headphones out of the cart as I reached for them. Then held them hostage over his head, and considering the bastard was almost six-five, I had no shot at getting them even if I jumped.

"Guy or girl?" He demanded and I huffed, exasperated.

"Guy. Satisfied?"

"Good or bad?"

"I already said it was fucking weird."

"Good then. So, what's the issue?" He yelped as I punched him in the armpit, snatching my headphones from his hand when his arm dropped.

"Let's just say we don't mix," I grumble, sliding them around my neck. "Now can we drop it?"

He sighs dramatically but lets it go. Half an hour later it's my turn to duck in the dressing room, knowing the girls are ready by now. As the resident gay guy, they've never minded. Even gave me my own little corner with a partition, and if we had the time, they would put eyeliner on me or other stuff. Tonight was one of those nights.

"Jackie!" Jenny was all glammed out, looking like a pixie and disco ball collided and had a love child. "Maria got this new mauve shade of cream shadow that you just *have* to—"

"Yep. But can I change my pants first?" A chorus of laughs as I ducked away, shrugging my leather jacket off.

I was painfully aware that I looked like I stepped right out of a 2009 skate park most days, so at work I liked to look a little different. Dress slacks, shiny shoes, and a reflective black button down. A bit more formal, but still not normal. That was the motto the girls had given me, and I had to admit it had a ring to it.

"Alright, what pink thing are you putting on me today?" I asked, plopping down in Jenny's chair. She and Maria crowded over me, repeating that it was mauve and yapping about what to do and something about hair gel, so I politely tuned out. I checked my phone for the last time while they fretted before having to turn it on silent for the night.

"What do you think?" Maria lifted my chin a few minutes later, and catching my reflection in the mirror I actually paused. Mauve was apparently darker than I predicted, similar to a light bruise. Paired with the bit of black liner it made my vacant green eyes seem deeper and bigger than normal. And then my hair. I don't know how the hell she did it, but it looked wet and

47

wavy all at once. I liked it a lot more than I was expecting.

"Honestly not bad. I might have you do this again, if it's not a hassle." Maria stood straight up and proud, hands patting my shoulders.

"I would love to."

"Now go have fun and try not to look like you want to kill everyone I talk to," Jenny adds with a laugh, pecking me on the cheek. I roll my eyes, but exit back to the stage with a bit more confidence than I had when coming in.

Ten minutes till go time, but the bouncers had already started letting people in. Seth let out a wolf whistle when he saw me, which I promptly responded to by flipping the bird. I still felt a grin tug at my mouth though, nerves settling for the first time in days.

Seth and I started a few minutes early, flicking the lights off and the strobes on. After easing the crowd in with an easy-to-follow techno beat, we hit the lasers and didn't slow down unless we needed water. I think he could tell I needed to work off excess energy because he was letting me take the lead more than normal. Rather than our usual back and forth, he was more of an MC for me rather than mixing beats himself.

And fuck I needed it, this natural high. The anxiety might have finally been quelled, by my confusion and frustration were still at a low boil. I poured it into the music, drop after drop, crest after crest, and the audience was loving it. At one point I saw some guy crowd surfing.

A hand waved in front of my face, Seth pulling me out of my stupor.

"What?" I shouted over the music, popping my headphones off one ear.

"It's almost midnight!" No shit. I yanked my sleeve up, checking my watch. "Go get a drink and sit for a while. We gotta push till two, and I don't need you crashing!"

I nodded, evening the beat out and slid out of the way. I hadn't felt it on stage but now that I moved more than just bobbing my head along to the music, my legs felt like freaking rubber.

Instead of disappearing backstage I weaved towards the bar instead. I needed a break, but I didn't want to abandon the atmosphere. This was the best I had felt in a long ass time, and I didn't want to risk losing it till the night was truly over.

With a Shirley Temple in hand, I leaned my back against the bar, letting my legs hang off the stool to stretch. The flash of the strobes was fainter over here, but the lasers still cut through enough to briefly blind me. I think that's why I didn't see him coming.

"Jackson?" I froze, slowly turning to my left and saw Carter standing there, staring at me slack jawed. Behind him I saw more of Heavens Boys and that had me moving. I left my half-finished drink on the bar, pushing straight into the crowd before they saw me.

"Nope." Carters voice cut into my ear, his hand already on my wrist and tugging me back between two people towards him.

"You can't make me disappear here!" I shouted over the music, and he tilted his head in question. I gestured up to the DJ booth frantically. "I'm at work. On a break."

The crowd swelled around us, pushing us closer together. I tried to keep some space, but he just slid his arms around my waist, pulling me flush against his chest.

"Can I occupy your break?" His voice was hot on my neck, sending another annoying shiver down my spine.

"For what?" I started shaking my head, but he caught my chin again, tilting my head to the side.

"...You look very nice like this." I felt myself gaping at him, and he grinned, the hand on my lower back pressing in. "Besides, we never got to finish our conversation the other day."

"I said not to touch me anymore," I argued, trying to twist out of his grip but he didn't let me run.

"Did you mean it?" His eyes were searching mine again, face highlighted by a slant of blue stage lights, making my breath catch. He found an answer in my silence, nodding once and leaning closer again. "This isn't the place to finish that conversation."

"...Fine." My heart felt like a wild thing in my chest as I pulled his hand off my face and turned the other way. "You get five minutes."

Chapter 5

Carter was looking at everything in my little dressing area. I thanked whatever god was looking down at me that I took the time to fold my other clothes and put them in my bag rather than tossing them haphazardly like normal.

"Well?" I snapped, my foot tapping the floor impatiently as he dragged a finger along the collar of my jacket hanging off the edge of the partition. He winced at my tone, eyes flicking to me.

"Sorry. Just taking it in."

"For?" I couldn't help my suspicions, but he chuckled, unoffended.

"I told you I want to help you, so I'm learning what I can." When I furrowed my brows he clarified, "Your fate lines. Even though I can't see them, I can still gently nudge you towards happiness if I learn enough."

"And why the hell does that matter to you?" I snip, and his face falls again, glancing away this time. He sounded like a damn wounded puppy when he said,

"Because it's my purpose."

Another bolt of guilt slashed through me, making me glance away too. I knew I was just being stubborn now, because like he said… I was afraid. I wasn't sure if I was ready to pursue anything, even if casual. Let alone explain my previous relationships. Especially not with a damn Cupid who seemed hell-bent on finding me love.

"Can you explain why you keep touching me then?" I finally mumble, focusing on the thrum of the distant bass rather than my anxiety. "How the hell it pertains to your so-called purpose."

He was in front of me in half a second, catching my hands in his.

"Yes." He lifted them till he could brush his mouth across my knuckles, instantly making me want to squirm again.

"Cupids are responsible for overseeing every form of love. Platonic. Romantic. Lustful." His eyes darkened slightly, voice dropping. "If I get a sense of what you physically like, which is arguably the easiest one to discover and understand, I can then urge you in a positive direction with less complications."

"And it has nothing to do with your own pleasure?" I grumble, narrowing my eyes at him. "Because earlier you looked..." I trailed off, swallowing hard.

"Looked like what?" His grin widened a fraction, tongue darting out against my fingers. I yanked my hands back instantly, making him chuckle.

"Stop acting like you're into it," I hissed, hands balling into fists at my sides. "Just because I'm gay doesn't mean you can—"

"First of all," he interrupts me smoothly, arms looping around my waist again. "I've already told you that I will stop if you tell me to stop." I clench my jaw, my frustration building again.

"And secondly..." His voice was like a purr against my neck as he spun us, backing me against the mirror on the wall slow enough that I could dart out if I wanted to. "I'm pansexual. So, I am very, genuinely, into it."

I felt my stomach flip as his mouth descended to my neck again, mimicking the same path it had in the café. My hands fisted the front of his shirt, chest burning from holding my breath, refusing to let any sounds out this time.

But then he had to go and suck on the soft space beneath my ear, and the breath I was stubbornly holding rushed out all at once.

"That's more like it." He grins down at me triumphantly, hands beginning to roam. "Tell me where you like to be touched, or I'll just guess."

"This entire situation is completely ridiculous," I mutter instead, my forehead dropping to his shoulder to hide my burning cheeks. He presses a gentle kiss on my temple, like a reassurance, before one of his hands pulls forward over my thigh, stroking me slowly.

My breathing hitched, as did Carters. Then a low laugh rumbled through his chest into mine. "You're already hard."

"Shut up," I growl, but he just hummed in response, his hand keeping up the gentle pressure against me.

"I'm not making fun of you," he reassures, his other hand cradling the back of my head. "It just pleases me immensely to feel how much you react to me. You don't strike me as a man who's easy."

That steadies me slightly. He would be the first to hold that opinion in a while, but I kept my mouth shut. Not like I trusted my voice at this point anyway; my breaths were already coming in gentle pants just from this.

"Can I touch you?" He whispers, voice coated with a need I felt building in my own blood. I grit my teeth, nodding my head against his chest. He tsked, tugging on my hair lightly, his hand over my cock pausing its movements entirely.

"I need to hear it." There was an unmistakable note of command in his tone now, a dominance leaking in that I didn't expect. But it wasn't unwelcome.

"Tch...yes. Yes, you can touch me," I whispered, ignoring the shake in my voice.

"Good boy." *Fuck.*

His hand in my hair tugged again, and this time I let him lean my head back, mouth meeting his as my eyes fell shut. When he kissed me, I felt it everywhere. I was too mad to acknowledge it the first time, but on edge like this, it was undeniable. His tongue played against mine, chest pressing me flat to the mirror at my back, and I let him drag me under.

One of my hands abandoned its death grip on his shirt to fist the hair at the nape of his neck. He instantly groaned into my mouth, the response sending a whip of satisfaction through me.

Finally, his hand slid against my length again, knee shoving between my legs with less patience than earlier. He made quick work of the button and zipper, mouth returning to my neck as he eased my cock out and into his palm. Then he stilled.

"What's this?" He asked, breathlessly. The pad of his thumb rolled purposefully over my tip, and my face flooded with a blush. How the hell did I forget?

"Um," I swallowed again, but nothing was going to keep my voice from shaking now. "A, uh, piercing. I got it pierced six years ago."

"So, you like a little bit of pain with your pleasure," he murmured, his voice damn near a growl.

Carefully he circled it, holding my head back so he could watch every tiny reaction I had. When the pad of his thumb rolled gently against the small metal ball, my hips jerked involuntarily, a rough gasp leaving me.

"Heh... understood." His mouth captured mine again before I could snap at him. This time when he stroked me, his palm deliberately dragging against the piercing, I couldn't hold back my moans anymore.

"Touch me too," he panted out, half an order and half a beg. He worked me faster when I pulled him down, sucking a kiss mark onto his skin just above his collar. I groaned roughly, tongue rolling across it again, chasing his infuriating sugary scent and taste.

"More," he rasped, and I yanked his shirt open, snapping the buttons clean off. Between my gasps my tongue traced his skin, teeth closing over his collarbone, hands reaching around behind him to squeeze his ass. His hips jerked into mine, his grip on me growing deliciously tighter, making me cry out.

"That's it baby, you're doing so good for me, being so honest." The praise just kept coming, making my moans tremble worse than before, my hips bucking into his palm.

"I'm- I- Carter." His name broke on my lips, but he shook his head, eyes flashing with something primal as he suddenly slowed his strokes. He caught my mouth in another kiss, swallowing the frustrated sob which tore out of me.

"If you're gonna cum from just my hand, then you're going to do it with me," he said hotly against my neck, free hand dragging mine down from his chest to his belt.

He kept stroking me torturously slow, squeezing my tip hard, thumb caressing my piercing until I had him in my hands. I could barely breathe as I gripped the root of him, desperately trying to match his pace.

He yanked on my hair again, sharp enough to make me whine this time. Pressing his lips to my ear, he thrust into my hand once, the tips of our cocks knocking together.

"Spit," he ordered on a whisper. Confusion barreled through me and he chuckled at the look on my face. He pressed one more hot kiss to my skin, ground his cock against mine again and growled out lower, "Spit. Or I stop."

I shuddered, squeezing my eyes shut against the embarrassment. After a moment of sucking on my tongue I opened my mouth, letting it drip out. We both shuddered as my saliva coated us, and the sound he let out against my neck made my cock throb even harder.

I couldn't keep pace with him anymore, having been at the edge for too long. All I could do was keep my grip on him as he thrust into my hand, stroking me in time with each of his rough bucks forward until I was crying out.

He stroked me straight through my release, knocking my piercing with the head of his cock on every thrust forward until he was spilling too. He gasped roughly in my ear, pressing a flurry of fervent kisses down my neck until we both finally stilled, ragged breaths echoing in the small space.

My legs were already weak when I'd gotten off stage. Now, they were damn near useless. I was only upright because of Carters hold on me.

Like he could feel that reliance, his hand left my hair to press against my lower back, steadying me. Wordlessly he plucked a few tissues out of the box on my dressing table, cleaning us both up while letting me hide my face against his shoulder again. Once my clothes were back into place, he exhaled softly atop my head.

"Talk to me Jackson," he murmured into my hair, a note of concern rising from beneath the lingering desire. "Did I hurt you?" I shook my head, and his hand on my back started rubbing slow, gentle circles again. He cleared his throat.

"Did you like it?"

I shut my eyes even though he couldn't see me. Coming down from the high, my thoughts began racing again, all loud and discombobulated. But there was one infinitely louder than the rest which I couldn't avoid anymore.

"Yes."

Chapter 6

I don't know how I dragged myself back onto that stage. My legs felt like stretched out rubber, my chest a gutted cavern, aching each time I breathed. Seth took one look at me and whatever complaint was rolling out of his mouth cut off. I knew I was gone for longer than a break, leaving him up here to sweat. As soon as the doors slammed shut against the last drunken group, my ass dropped straight to the damn floor, elbows braced on my knees.

"Dude you gotta tell me what's going on." He was already squatting in front of me, holding out a bottle of water. "I'm beginning to worry here."

"I'm fine," I grumble, but take the bottle, downing half of it. He narrowed his eyes at me, but I cut him off before he could press. "I'm not in danger, I'm not flying off the rail, and I don't wanna talk about it."

"You don't wanna talk about the frat guy I saw dragging you across the dance floor?" Seth asked anyway, fixing me with the Dad stare he usually gave the girls. I heaved a sigh, not bothering to deny it.

"What frat guy?" Seth and I both jumped, gazes finding Jenny who was standing at the top of the stairs, halfway between confused and concerned.

"Just Carter!" I blurt out, pleading for her to roll with it through my eyes. Her brow ticks, eyes narrow, but she tosses her hair, and I sigh in relief.

"Who's Carter?" Seth asks, glancing between the two of us.

"Classmate."

"Colleague."

Seth glanced between the pair of us skeptically and I shot Jenny another look. He could *not* find out that Carter was the guy from my not-school-shooting freakout, or he would try to kill him. He was like that with everyone who stressed me out after the crap that happened in my senior year.

Jenny was glaring right back at me but must have finally caught the desperation I was feeling, and relented.

"He's a harmless undergrad," she finally said with another perfectly bored sigh. "Too invested in the social life and was probably stunned to see we work here is all."

"More like stunned to see me dolled up like a twink," I muttered, forcing myself to roll with it, dropping my head back down in exhaustion. "We all know I don't usually dress this…"

"Glamourous," Jenny supplied, her heels clicking as she made her way over to me. "You were great tonight as always, but I'm driving because you look like hell and I have a very important test tomorrow."

Monday. Fuck me.

I dragged myself to my feet, packing up sloppier than normal, and didn't bitch at Seth when he grabbed my cart to roll it down to the parking garage. He went ahead, leaving me and Jenny to step in the elevator alone. And she pounced immediately.

"Your hair was all messed up and your makeup was smudging under your eyes. More than your usual from sweating and dancing around up there." I grit my teeth, but she elbowed me.

"Jesus, fine." I rubbed the sore spot on my ribs, heaving a breath. "We didn't fuck backstage so get your mind out of the gutter."

"But?"

"...he mighta gotten me off."

My throat felt dried out again as the elevator dinged, but neither of us moved to get off, the doors whooshing slowly shut again. I avoided looking at our blurred reflections in the stainless steel, knowing she was staring at me, trying to work it out.

"That would be the first time you let anyone touch you since Andrews. Right?" She asked it so gently, but I still felt like a bomb went off in my gut. I could only nod sharply, and she slid her arm around my waist. "Oh Jackie..."

"I'm fine god damn it," I mutter, but wrap an arm around her shoulders anyway, sinching her tight to my side.

It had been almost four years since Andrews. I'd been the younger one then, with less experience and riding the high of actually catching a guy's attention for once. Made me blind to all the red flags, which in retrospect should have been easy to spot since he was my damn advisor. I was just in denial.

"I'm assuming you're okay with whatever you two did, since Carter didn't stumble out with any busted or bloody limbs?" I huffed a laugh, shaking my head.

"I am not giving you any details," I say, pushing the button for the doors again and this time we step out, still arm in arm.

"At least tell me if you think you're going to see him again or not," she pouted, tugging on me gently.

"It's not like this was planned to begin with. He was just... here." She plucked my keys out of my hand as soon as I fished them out of my pocket. Frowning, I caved, sliding into the passenger seat. I was fucking beat.

"Why him though? Is he holding some type of grudge or leverage since you called the cops on him?" Concern had worked its way back in her voice, and I shook my head quickly.

"No, it's nothing like that."

Thinking back on it, Carter hadn't seemed mad at all. A little confused, placating, but even when I stormed his dorm room the first time we kissed, he'd just let me yell. Any normal person would

74

have gotten a restraining order against me at the very least. But with this whole Cupid thing spiraling out of control, he just kept tracking me down.

"If you think it's something you're going to pursue," Jenny interrupted my racing thoughts with that tone of hers that told me I was going to hate the next thing coming out of her mouth. "You need to tell Carter. Because from what I've seen, he actually seems to like you despite how you met."

"It's not like that," I say again, shaking my head. I didn't even know how to begin explaining to her what he was and his claims about my fate lines or whatever. I still only half believed it myself.

"Fine," she huffed, swerving the car out of the lot and onto the road. "But you'll tell me if that changes?"

"Always," I whisper, and she settles.

Half an hour later I'm staring at my dorm ceiling, low trap beats echoing from the headphones lying on my chest. I had three and a half more months till graduation, and Cupid or not, Carter was still just a twenty-two-year-old kid. I would just be a confusing blip in his life, before disappearing completely.

Chapter 7

It was fucking freezing, even for New England standards. The wind whipping my face didn't even give my breath time to cloud in front of me as I trudged along, clinging to my iced coffee for dear life. I had a text from Jenny when I woke up, half dead and aching all over. She said something about a hat and gloves, the latter I was lucid enough to grab at least.

Half of this was my own damn fault. Every semester I signed up for eight a.m.'s, wanting my afternoons and evenings for myself. Helped a lot with the DJ gigs since I could get a nap in. Here I was thinking of naps when there's a kid jogging towards me at seven fifty in the morning.

"Hey, excuse—" I furrowed my brows when he didn't even glance at me. His paced stayed steady, and I nearly dropped my coffee in the piles of slush lining the sidewalk as I dodged. "...me," I finished awkwardly at his retreating back. He hadn't seen me?

He hadn't seen me.

I was suddenly very awake and alert, a small pump of adrenaline warming my frozen muscles. I immediately glanced to the roof of the language arts building, but it was empty, confusing me further. Maybe it was just a coincidence.

Nope, that false hope evaporated when a group of girls crashed into my back, giggling and blaming each other for tripping as they continued on. My eyes scanned the roof of the library, the business school, and the auditorium. Nothing. As my frustration mounted I finished my coffee, stuffing my hands into my pockets. Then I felt a prickle at the back of my neck, and stiffened.

That's right... Carter had left a mark on me. And through the frigid air, that spot on my skin was warm. I turned, glancing over my shoulder and the mark warmed further as my gaze scanned the windows, finally spotting him on the second floor of the library in one of the wide windows.

My stomach lurched seeing the crossbow in his hands. I couldn't help it. After two decades of active shooter drills it was an automatic response.

I shuffled off the main path so not to get run into again, watching. I was curious of how it worked. He'd explained the threads and the functionality of it, but I was curious if I could *see* it. And he didn't seem to notice me yet, so I let myself stare.

There were no arrows on the bow as he peered through the scope, a lock of his hair falling against his forehead. A flicker of a smile on his lips. I grit my teeth, eyes back on the bow.

His hand raised, making a plucking motion like my mother used to make when getting leaves out of my hair as a kid. A sharper tug, a flash of red.

My stomach flipped as the thread appeared, pulled taut and poised, his finger drifting to the trigger. It passed through the glass and flew over my head soundlessly. I whipped around, watching as it sinks into the back of a girl's neck. Unnervingly, in the same place of the mark he'd left on me.

It looked like she had just spilled her books everywhere coming down the staircase. And the kid that was jogging towards me earlier had skidded to a stop, squatting to help her. He said something that made her laugh, their fingers brushing as he passed a folder back to her.

I couldn't help but snort. Classic.

The mark on the back of my neck prickled again and I looked back up at the window. Carter was gone though, and when I huffed an annoyed breath a group of students passing me jumped, like I'd appeared from thin air.

As I was debating whether or not to duck into the library to see if I could find him, the belltower chimed at five of the hour. I cursed, decision made for me as I began speedwalking towards the creative arts center. The prof of this class was a stickler. If you weren't there by eight, your ass was locked out.

I slid into my seat, flushed and somehow sweating despite the cold with one minute to spare. He arched a brow at me as he passed my desk, clicking the lock into place, but didn't chastise me.

For the first time in a while my classes dragged. My gaze kept tugging towards the doors and windows, searching for Carter against my will. It was embarrassing, in a way. One decent hand job and here I was searching for him with goo goo eyes.

No... I shouldn't chastise myself like that. What we'd done went a hell of a lot deeper than the physicality, trudging up memories I'd worked hard to bury. I gripped my pencil hard to keep my hand from shaking, trying to calm my racing nerves with a few measured breaths.

"You look warmer than earlier." I stiffened, feeling the chair next to mine pull out, the scent of sugar invading my space. Carters knee knocked against mine but I didn't respond, paying attention to the prof

82

for the first time today like my life depended on it.

"You were watching me this morning." Damn it.

"Can't blame me. I almost got trampled because of you," I muttered gruffly and he chuckled.

"Sorry about that. I didn't expect you to be up so early. Thought it was safe."

"I have eight a.m.'s every Monday, Wednesday and Friday." I could feel his eyes on me as I scribbled something useless in my notebook. "So just... give me a heads up," I add, quieter.

"Oh?" he props his chin in his hand, leaning close enough that I can feel his breath on my cheek. "Does that mean I can finally get your number?"

I pause again, jaw setting against the warmth rising in my cheeks. Cheeky bastard.

"Fine," I grumble and pull my phone out of my bag, passing it to him. His fingers needlessly drag against the back of my hand before he takes it.

Maybe I was wrong with some of my claims to Seth. Giving a Cupid who I was connected to by a magic kiss mark my cell number seemed like a move only a spiraling guy would make.

"Who's A?"

I stop breathing, the world going quiet around me. I can't hear anything but my rampant heartbeat.

Andrews. The text messages. I'm stupid, so fucking stupid I—

"Jackson." Doe eyes, warm hands. "Breath," Carter whispers, gaze steady, cupping my face. "With me."

My throat feels like it's being crushed as I wrench a breath in, force it out. Slowly, Carter leans his forehead against mine, one of his hands seeking mine out and pulling it flat to his chest. His heartbeat is a little rushed, but his breaths are steady. In, out, in, out.

The pain in my chest slowly unravels, and I sag in my seat. I don't fight him as he shifts for me to lean my weight into his side. For once, his insistent teasing had quelled, staying quiet and patient as I collect myself.

Class must have ended because when I finally glance up, we're the only ones left. Or maybe he did some crazy Cupid thing and made everyone leave with his fate magic or something. Whatever. I was just glad to not have an audience as I dragged myself away from the edge of a breakdown. Again.

"Do you have panic attacks often?" Carter asks gently, still holding me. I shake my head, embarrassment beginning to tinge the edges of my anxiety. But I still don't want to pull away. This was the fastest one stopped, and I didn't want to lose the bubble of calm his presence somehow provided.

"I don't know," I finally murmur, throat raw. Probably more than the average person, but not as bad as a few years ago.

"Hm." He cups my cheek again, presses a feather light kiss to one of my own, then leans back. "Do you want to talk about this person?"

"No." My entire body clenches and unclenches, but the bolt of panic I was expecting doesn't come.

I don't want to look at him. Whether he's curious or concerned doesn't matter. I've endured enough people trying to force feed me their version of 'help' over the years, and the dynamic between us was already confusing enough as it was.

"Look, Carter," I start, my hands fisting in my lap. "I know you think you're helping me, but I really—"

"Obviously I'm not helping you." My gaze shoots over to him, confusion coursing through me.

Rather than looking at me with that sense of sympathy I've grown to hate, he looked downright pissed. His knee was bouncing, jaw set as he stared down at the desk in front of us, hard. "In fact, I think I've only been making it worse for you so far."

"What?" I can't hide the shock in my voice, eyes following him as he stands up.

"I've been obsessed with why I can't see your fate lines," he says, frustration and a hint of guilt evident in his voice. "So much so that I haven't been paying attention to anything you might be going through. I've just been so aggravated that I can't do for you what I can for everyone else that I've been pushy and insensitive. I'm sorry."

I didn't know what to say for a minute, my heart a wild thing in my chest. From my perspective, other than Jenny, he's paid more attention to my habits and emotions than anyone else had in years. I didn't know if his guilt was stemming from the physical interactions we've had, but if so it wasn't necessary. Even when he was pursuing me like that, he was paying attention, communicating, making me feel seen and heard.

And the sudden realization of that terrified me more than anything else, because this was temporary.

"Look," I start again, clearing my throat awkwardly as I felt the blush rising in my cheeks. "You need to get over yourself."

It was his turn to look down at me confused and I winced. He looked like a freaking scolded puppy, again.

"Stop pouting." I huff as I stand, finally gathering my crap to hide the shaking in my hands.

"I'm obviously not a guy who gets sappy with others, but that doesn't mean I want to see you squirm like this either. If you think you're hurting me or failing at your Cupid duties or any other stupid crap like it, stop. As far as I'm concerned you're not responsible for any of my issues. And..."

I trailed off, zipping my bag up. Damn it, this was embarrassing.

"And?" He prodded gently, his brief dejectedness already shifting to something more excited again. I swear if this guy had a tail, it would be wagging like crazy right now.

"And it's not like I've hated anything you've been doing," I admit begrudgingly. Then I surprise myself by releasing a quiet laugh, shaking my head. "You're actually the first guy I've let into my life, let alone touch me since... A. So, even though you've been pushy like you said, you are helping. A little bit, at least."

His hundred-watt smile was back in place, but I ducked out from under him before he could wrap me up in his arms. He protested instantly, whining at my heels but I just pulled my hood up to cover my blush as I shoved out the auditorium room door.

Less than a foot into the hallway he slid a hand into mine again, not stopping me but matching pace and keeping me close with a content hum. I kept my gaze on the floor, not wanting to see if anyone was looking at us. All I needed was the rumor mill starting up again, this time painting me as a pervert for going for an underclassmen. Funny how no one painted Andrews as that when he was the older guy. I was just a slut for sleeping with a prof.

"You have that look on your face again like you're ready to fight the world." Carter's voice was quiet in my ear and I jolted, heat flooding through me as I jerked my head away.

"Jesus dude." I tossed another glare at him but he only laughed again.

"Tell me what you're thinking in that pretty little head of yours."

"Nothing."

"Liar." He was looking at me expectantly again, so open and curious that for a beat, I considered explaining who A was to him. But then the rushed thought of how it would affect him struck me quiet again.

He was a Cupid. His purpose, as he said, was helping people find positive, loving relationships with one another. I didn't want to know what look he would give me if he knew how bad my last one had turned out. So instead, I forced a disgruntled sigh, voicing the comparison that my stupid brain regularly made to try and get the attention off of me for a damn minute.

"That you're like a dog," I grumble, walking faster. "I keep imagining droopy ears when you're sad because you freaking pout, or a tail wagging a million miles an hour when you're stupidly happy about something."

When I sneak a glance at him, he looks surprised. There's even a bit of color rising in his own cheeks, before he catches me looking and laughs again. I tick a brow. Interesting, the guy could be embarrassed like the rest of us.

I roll my thumb over his knuckles experimentally as we step outside, feeling his hand twitch in mine. Shift slightly closer as the bitter wind hits us, his body automatically relaxing against mine as he drops my hand to slide his arm around my waist. Eager to touch me. Eager to please.

I pushed a little further, ignoring the tip taps of anxiety and adrenaline in my chest as I reached up, pulling his hood over his head too. The tint of color in his cheeks darkens further, and I finally smirk.

"See? Look at you. Despite your momentary dominance last night, you act like a freaking puppy, wanting all my attention." That pouts on his face again and it's my turn to laugh, a true sound coming out of me for once.

He groans low, embarrassment rolling him in waves. But whatever nerves I'd hit must jolt him into action. His arm on my waist tightens suddenly, yanking me flush to his side. His nose skims my cheek, hot breath sliding beneath my hood, making me shudder.

"H-hey. People can see—"

"Woof." It's a whisper against my skin but rocks through me all the same. He doesn't budge, doesn't let up his hold on me either as I force my arms between us and try to shove him off. My attempt is further cut off when his tongue darts out against my cheek, and I feel myself go up in flames.

He lets out a hushed, satisfied sound by my response, tilting his head back slightly to look at me with a smirk of his own. "Want me to bark for real this time?"

"You're insane!" He laughs heartily at my outburst, but let's me shove him off this time. I pull my hood further up over my face as I start speed walking back towards the dorms, but his hand gripping my wrist halts my retreat.

"Let me take you on a date," he offers, grinning at me as I glare up at him. Then adds, voice unmistakably suggestive, "Somewhere you can blow off some steam."

"Carter," I growl out, voice low with warning but his grin just widens as it always does.

"Cross my heart and hope to die, I promise it's pure of heart." My own heart flips in my chest again, body and mind at different places and I'm unable to keep up with either.

"...When?" I finally mumble out, still pissed he managed to embarrass me again but... fuck, I wanted to go. I wanted to do something with him other than be embarrassed by his touches and comments, something other than yelling at him to keep myself safe.

Oblivious to my inner turmoil he nuzzles the top of my head through the hood, subtly pulling my face to hide in his neck as another group of students approach us. That alone makes my heart ache. Such a prick, but so freaking protective without me needing to ask.

"I'm free right now if you are."

Chapter 8

I offered to drive but Carter insisted on taking his own car. Said something vague about not wanting me to be an unsafe driver in case his plans exhausted me. That solicited enough embarrassment for me to scramble in the passenger seat and slam the door shut before he could say something even more pervy.

The radio hummed in the small space comfortably, making the uncommon silence between us a bit more bearable. And was something for me to focus on other than his hand on my thigh which he refused to move. The relaxed touch grew firmer every time I tried to pry his fingers off, so eventually I just gave up.

"The mall?" I couldn't decide if I thought it was funny or annoying for him to take me to such a basic first date place. But as he all but bounced around the outside of the car to open my door, I bit my tongue.

"Not a shopping trip, I promise," he said, reading my mind as I stepped out, staring up at the building skeptically. "Just trust me."

His hand was in mine again before I could argue, and again I kept my head down as he steered me inside. It wasn't like I cared what people thought of me and him together. I just didn't want the wrong people to see me with a guy again. My life had finally begun to even out before Carter showed up and bulldozed through what foundations I'd begun to re-lay. And my weak ass was letting him.

"Here we are!" I glanced up at the shop we'd stopped in front of. 'Jerry's Rage Room. Fun for all.'

"I don't get it," I said, but let him pull me through the doors anyway. The shop was darker than the others, bigger too, with hallways disappearing off to the side like a movie theater. He shifted his hand to my lower back as we approached the counter, his million-watt smile making the girl at the register blush instantly. At least I wasn't the only one.

"Hello." Carter leaned against the counter, tilting his head just so. That lock of hair curled against his forehead, and the left side of his mouth curved into a wickedly insufferable grin which made my knees weak even though it was aimed at her. "If you have any open rooms we'd like two tickets, please."

"Well, I'm supposed to stay closed till my managers back from lunch," she says, a nervous giggle coming from her. I narrowed my eyes slightly as she twirled a lock of her own hair around her finger, her gaze on Carter darkening slightly. "But he should be back at any minute so I guess I could let you in a bit early."

"That would be fabulous," Carter says, his wallet already out. "How much do I owe ya cutie?"

I stood there with my jaw clenched as they flirted back and forth, body prickling with something dangerously close to jealousy. I didn't like the way she looked at him, didn't like how easily she gave us her employee discount, and outright hated the way her hips swayed as she walked ahead of us down the hall, unlocking one of the rooms.

"You get an uninterrupted twenty minutes," she says, holding the door open for us. "There's a panic button on the wall in case of an injury or... anything else you might need." I needed a bucket to throw up in.

"Thank you so much sweetheart. I'll be sure to keep an eye on the clock so we don't get you in trouble." She outwardly preened as Carter flashed her a wink, the door finally shutting between us.

"What the hell was that?" The words burned in my throat. I shrugged out of my jacket more aggressive than necessary and chucked it against one of the chairs lining the wall. Carter arched a brow as he slid his own coat off deliberately slower.

"Just me working some of my magic. We saved forty bucks." His eyes lit up, leaning a fraction closer. "Don't tell me a little flirting made you jealous, Jackson?"

"Like hell," I muttered, glancing around the room. There was a table lined with glass bottles and a few pairs of safety goggles and gloves. A bat, a hammer. A freaking bed of a truck. "What the hell am I looking at?"

"You've never heard of a rage room before?" I grit my teeth but shook my head. Maybe. Never looked into them though. Carter rested his hands on my shoulders, thumbs gently working against my tense muscles.

"You're allowed to break everything in here. A physical outlet for stress, or trauma." He said it softly, like he knew the reaction he would get from me. A wave of paranoia, and defensiveness. Panic that I was getting so sick of feeling. He kissed the top of my head.

"I'm not expecting you to explain yourself. But I'm also not going to pretend that you're not hurting either. I thought this could help."

My heart clenched again. Why. Why did he have to be so God damn nice, so aware. I glanced at the table again, weighing my options. I could refuse, and feel like shit as always. Or I could try it, even if it was ridiculous.

"For the record, I think this is stupid," I say bluntly as I step out from under his touch and snatch a pair of goggles. Then pick up one of the bottles, tossing it lightly between my hands. Toss it against the wall opposite of me, and wince when it thuds on the floor, barely cracked.

"Harder." I glance at Carter annoyed, but he's dead serious. He takes a seat in one of the chairs, leans back and gets comfortable. I scoff, but pick up another bottle, throwing it with purpose this time.

A different type of adrenaline seeps through my veins when this one shatters into a million pieces, glass skittering across the floor. In any other setting this would be bad. Considered a breakdown. A step backwards. But here I'm literally supposed to break this shit instead of myself.

I'm panting lightly by the time all the bottles are scattered across the floor, the shards of glass glinting in sloppy piles. Carter whistles and I flip him off, picking up the bat. Stare down the dented bed and bumper. Briefly I wondered how many other people have taken hits at it, and why they needed to.

I glance back at Carter, expecting some variation of judgement or concern on his face but find the opposite. His gaze was hot on mine, cheeks slightly flushed. Then a smirk, a wink at me this time, somehow sexier than the one he afforded the girl. It's all the permission I need.

I slam the bat into the tailgate, the ricochet reverberating up my arms, but I don't care. I bring it down again and again, shattering what's left of the tail light, snapping the plastic fender clean off and denting the metal beneath. All the anger I've wrapped myself in, that I'd grown high around me to keep the pain out, explodes in this room and on this stupid truck.

I was in a blind fury until the snap of wood echoed over the bang against the metal. I'd snapped the damn bat, half the barrel skidding across the floor leaving me with a mangled stick. I chuck it into the bed of the truck, bracing my hands on my knees and gasping for breath.

My ears ring in the sudden quiet, vision blurring against tears I don't want to let fall. Fucking Andrews, the piece of shit. I don't give a damn that he was fired, it wasn't enough. He deserved worse than the slap on the back of the hand the state gave him. He didn't even get any fucking community service after what he did to me.

"Jackson..." Carter's voice eases through the rage and grief. I can feel his hands hovering over me, holding himself back like I'm the closest to breaking he's ever seen me. I'm never fucking breaking again.

I whirl, a hand catching him by the back of his neck and yank his mouth to mine. His body tenses with a moment of hesitation, before melting into mine with equal fury.

That's what I was still feeling right now. Fury. It was too big, been weighing me down too long, and now I was using him as my outlet. And fucking hell he was letting me.

I work him backwards, slamming him into the wall hard enough to make him gasp. Break the kiss briefly to throw the goggles away and then my hands trap him against me. My touch slides up from his hips, under his shirt and over his ribs.

He groans the instant I draw my tongue over his lower lip, demanding more of him. Then I gasp at the bite of pain as he fists my hair and angles me back, taking control of the kiss as his tongue graces my open mouth. His free hand yanks me forward possessively, hips bucking against mine the second that we're close enough, forcing a heady breath out of me.

A few more shaky steps and he's dropping back into the chair, dragging me down onto his lap. I straddle him easily, rolling against him rougher than he had before, my anger giving way to my need. I don't hold back my moans this time when his mouth drifts to my neck, biting and sucking, less careful than he was last night.

My neck is throbbing with his kiss marks, my cock aching for his touch, for relief from this. But after sucking one more mark into my skin, he pulls back, hands locking on my hips and holding me still.

"Jackson—"

"Please," I huff out and his eyes widen. I felt like I was possessed as I lean in again, licking a stripe up his neck, sucking a mark into his skin which he shudders through.

"Baby," he tries again, and I lock the desperate whine in my throat, grinding down against him again despite the hold he has on me. He curses low, hands leaving my hips to grip my ass.

"You want me that bad?" His voice is low, demanding, making a delicious lick of heat curl through me.

"Yes," I huff out, face burning but I don't care. I need it. I need this. I need *him*. His pupils are blown so wide his eyes are nearly black, one of his hands shifting from my ass to my belt but a crackle of static has us both freezing.

"Gentle five-minute warning." The girl at the front desk, a giggle in her voice. I drop my head to Carter's shoulder, humiliation coursing through me as I remember where we are. His arms wrap around me protectively though, a hand keeping me pressed close against the back of my neck.

"Thanks sweetheart," he calls out the response, rough and rushed. One more pop of static, and then silence again.

"Jackson?" His fingers press into the back of my neck gently, trying to coax me out but I bury deeper against him. "You don't have to be embarrassed."

"I'm not!" I snap, heaving out a frustrated breath. "I'm... just trying to calm down."

"You're not the only one," he admits, heaving a sigh of his own. I shift to get off him, but he yanks me back, burying his face in my neck for a moment and just breathing me in. And I felt wholly relaxed for the first time in three years.

This time when I shift back, he lets me go. I don't want to know what I look like. I can still feel the imprint of his mouth on my neck, and when I run my hands through my hair my fingers get caught on knots which weren't there before.

Sliding my jacket back on I glanced back over at him, finding him watching me again. I grit my teeth.

"What?" He just smirks, tosses his own jacket over his shoulder, and opens the door with a dramatic sweep of his arm.

"Shall we?"

The girl that worked here was just as bubbly as before but this time, I'm less bothered by her. Carters arm is around my waist again, but his hand is dipped into the back pocket of my jeans. It was just... there. An intimate, but reassuring touch as he flirted our way out the door.

My own hands were stuffed in the front pockets of my jeans, trying to hide the fact that I was still half hard. I don't know what came over me back there. Maybe it was just the adrenaline. But Carter's lack of judgement certainly left a deciding mark on the moment. A hyper burst of clarity made me realize if we hadn't been interrupted, I really would have done it with him.

I glanced at him, yapping about something that I wasn't paying attention to. I was distracted by his sugary scent. The smile which curved his lips. The brightness in his eyes. He was so young. Unhurt. And this was a job. That had been made clear to me more than once, and kidding myself into believing it was something more than a young, stubborn Cupid taking me under his metaphorical wing on an odyssey to find me happiness would just hurt me later. But still...

A dark thought flickered to life as I slid back into the car, dumping my head against the headrest. Andrews hadn't just broken my heart; he'd obliterated my entire life. Maybe that's why Carter couldn't see any fate lines potentially connecting me to other people. Maybe I was so broken, he wouldn't be able to succeed at what he was trying to do for me.

And my delusional heart considered... Maybe instead of searching for someone else for me, he would stay.

Chapter 9

My body was too hot, the blankets sliding against me feeling more like weights. I still fisted them anyway, burying my face to muffle my cries. Harder. He was going harder. I wasn't ready for it, but God I wasn't going to tell him to stop.

"You're so much better than my wife, you know that right, Jackson?" A sob tore out of me as my head was yanked back, my back arching at a severe angle. "Say it," he growled out.

"I'm better than your wife." The words tumbled out of me, sloppy and desperate.

"Fuck." He pinned me facedown, hand gripping the back of my neck so hard

I couldn't breathe. My vision went white at the edges as he fucked me harder, deeper. "My perfect student, and perfect little cock sleeve."

Jackson.

Jackson.

"Jackson?"

My eyes flew open, a gasp tearing out of me as I sat up. One hand automatically went to my throat, feeling my racing pulse under my grip. The other was fisted in the blankets pooled around my waist. Blankets that... weren't mine.

"Morning," Carter murmured, voice thick and groggy with sleep. He sat up behind me, pressing a few lazy kisses across my bare shoulder as I took stock of what the hell was going on.

I could see my jacket hung up on the back of the door in front of me. I didn't know where my shirt was and based on what I could feel my jeans were gone too. My hand in the blankets flew to my crotch, breathing out a sigh of relief once I confirmed my boxers were still on.

"You okay?" Carter finally stopped kissing my skin to rest his chin on my shoulder. "You were moaning in your sleep. Not fun moans."

Images of the dream flashed through my mind again. Half made my gut twist again, but the louder half was relieved as I realized that's all that it was. Just a dream. Nothing bad happened. But I was still almost naked in Carters bed.

"Perverted brat!" I snap, finding my wits and grabbing a pillow. Carter lets out a dramatic 'oof' when I swing, whacking him in the face with it. He falls back to the mattress without a fight, groaning against the pillow as I smother him with it.

"Do I get a chance to explain before you try to kill me?" He asks, voice muffled, but I could still tell he was laughing.

"No." I was still far too embarrassed to even consider what happened here.

"Jaaacksooon," he calls out, hands settling on my hips, pulling me down against him. "I'm really starting to get lightheaded here."

I mutter a curse, pulling the pillow back far enough for him to breathe, but still stuffed between us so I could hide. His—*bare*—chest swells underneath me as he takes a breath, and I sink further into the pillow, mind reeling.

"Explain," I demand, my patience shot already.

"You fell asleep on the car ride back. I wasn't really surprised since you'd worked the night before and then beat the shit out of that truck." His fingers started tracing slow circles against my lower back, like he's trying to calm me down.

"My clothes?" I snip, not letting it go yet and he chuckles.

"Folded on my desk. I know from experience sleeping in a leather jacket and jeans doesn't always par well with the body."

"Of course you do," I grumble, sneaking a peek at him over the pillow. His eyes are glittering with humor, but then soften slightly.

"How did you sleep?"

"Woulda slept better in my own bed." I force the complaint, my heart still skipping around like an unhinged teenagers. Carter's fingers pause on my skin, a flash of hurt in his eyes.

"I didn't know where your dorm was. And it was late, so I just thought…"

"Stop," I murmur, hiding my face again. "I'm not actually mad. I was just caught off guard."

"Oh? So, you don't mind sleeping with me?" Carter chuckled low as I started to squirm again. One of his arms looped around my waist, pinning me to him as he successfully yanks my pillow-shield away and tosses it to the floor.

I open my mouth to argue but he doesn't let me, hand pressing to the nape of my neck, pulling me down for a kiss. Soft, slow, lazy morning. Like he has all the time in the world with me.

I relax against him a fraction, and he hums his approval, hand smoothing up my spine till both are gripping my hair gently. Goosebumps alight on my skin, a rush going through my nervous system, but I tilt my head, angling into him. After a few more breathless minutes he relaxes back, eyes half lidded as he traces my jawline.

"So... can we talk about yesterday?"

"What about it?" He ticks a brow at my question, a smirk twitching the corner of his mouth.

"Well specifically, I want to know everything I did to not only get you in my lap, but also to get you to grind against me that enthusiastically." My jaw goes slack and he chuckles, not done with his teasing yet. He pushes up on an elbow, lips ghosting over my ear as he whispers, "I would like to repeat it as often as possible."

"Ugh, you little—"

"Yo Carter!"

My mouth snaps shut simultaneously with his smirk evaporating. Footsteps thump towards his door at far more rapid of a rate than I can react to. Where the hell do I go? Under the covers? The bed? The closet?

I have one foot on the floor when Carter grabs me again, yanking me back into his lap. His arm locks around my waist, chest strong against my back as his free hand clamps over my mouth before I can shout.

I freeze again as the door swings open. One of Heavens Boys leans into the frame, peering around the room confused. He's not even looking at us, like we're not even there.

I relax slightly against Carter, realizing he must be pulling his Cupid shit right now. Still, my stomach does a backflip as the guy glances at my clothes, but then he's turning away and the breath I was holding releases silently.

"Yo Zach?" He calls back out into the hall, still lingering in the doorway. "You see Carter leave yet today?"

As the two idiots begin to bicker about who saw what, I crane my neck back to try and meet Carter's eye, and my entire body stalls at the look on his face.

I've never seen him glare before, so the heat behind it made my gut clench. Not only that but his jaw was set so hard it looked chiseled from rock, his upper lip pulled back in what I could only describe as a snarl. Territorial. That's what it felt like as his grip on me clenched tighter, drawing me into him until I was dwarfed by his larger frame.

My heart wasn't racing anymore, not like it usually did. It was beating steady, but hard. Drumming my awareness into my skull whether I could handle it or not.

He could have just grabbed my wrist, held a finger up to his own mouth to warn me to be quiet. Okay maybe the covering my mouth idea was sound because I had been about to shout and start blubbering excuses, but the rest of this was...

The door finally shut, leaving us in relative silence. I could hear some trap beats off in the distance which I guess was normal for a frat house even this early. But the thing was, I couldn't listen to the music like normal.

Typically, I could cling to it, let it drown everything else out. But right now, the only sounds my brain was capable of tracking were the deeper breaths Carter was pulling in a fraction away from my neck. The subtle creak of the headboard as he leaned back against it. And the steady beat of his heart pounding against my spine.

His hand had fallen from my mouth, arms now loosely wrapped around my waist and shoulders. Forehead drooping against the back of my head, hanging onto me until he could calm down. I'd been there enough to realize what was happening. I just didn't understand why it was happening to him now.

"I'm sorry," he mumbled, his breath rolling down my spine and I fought the urge to stiffen.

"There's nothing to apologize for. You... did the smartest thing," I admit, ignoring the way my voice came out lighter than normal. If he hadn't gone Cupid mode, this would have been a hell of a situation to explain to his frat brothers. Especially if any of them recognized who I was.

"Not for that."

"Huh?" I tried to glance back at him again, but he held me tighter, legs coming up on either side of me and this time I did stiffen. "Carter—"

"I can't take it anymore." His voice was hot in my ear, the tremble in his words making my mouth slam shut. Then drop open again on a shocked *'ah'* as his mouth closed on the nape of my neck, sucking hard.

"I never want to let my marks on you fade." The statement was half a growl, half a whisper which made my toes curl. "I never want *anyone* else to see you like this. I wouldn't be able to handle it."

He flipped us faster than any human could, his usual gentleness with me evaporating into something both desperate and demanding. He didn't bother trying to hold his weight off me, settling himself between my legs as his mouth continued its assault on my neck. A moan slipped out of me before I could stop it, my hands fisting the blankets as he rolled his hips just right.

"Carter," I gasped out, trying to get him to pause. I needed to understand; I couldn't just throw myself into this. My hand cupped his cheek, but he snatched it with one of his, fingers lacing with mine as he pins it down.

"Hey." I force some annoyance back into my voice and buck up against him, hard. "Look at me, puppy."

He froze, mouth hovering over my abdomen for half a second, before his gaze whipped up to meet mine. Dark, and daring. A brewing dominance which my attitude provoked.

"Why did you apologize?" He scoffs, turning his attention back to my body but I yank his hair with my free hand, making him hiss. "Answer or get the fuck off of me."

"Because I don't want to fucking help you anymore!" He surged over me, caging me in under him as his hands slammed down on either side of my head. His eyes were wild and dark, cheeks flushing, and voice growing rougher by the second.

"Do you have any idea what you're doing to me? I'm terrified every time I see you that a fate line will finally appear because I don't want you connected to anyone else but me. I don't want to have to let you go, I don't want to have to see you happy with someone else, because I want you to be mine!"

Shock and desire twisted through me, the latter he somehow recognized in my expression because he descended on me again. Our mouths moved in tandem, breaths and gasps molding together and drowning the world out. My back arched as he guided my legs higher, fingers deftly dragging my boxers off before spreading against my skin, like he was committing my shape to memory.

"Jackson," he groaned out against my shoulder. "If you don't tell me to stop—"

"Shut up," I hissed, my fingers slinking down his torso and hooking in the waistband of his sweatpants. Before I could go any further he slid down my body, a hand curving under my ass to lift me to him as his tongue flattened against the head of my cock.

My head fell back to the mattress instantly, hands covering my face as a whimper slipped out of me. He didn't let me hide this time, his free hand reaching up to lace our fingers before pinning it beside my hip.

I didn't know if it was because it had been so long, or because it was him, but I couldn't stay quiet any longer. Especially not as his tongue deliberately teased my piercing before taking me deeper.

I could only try to stifle the broken moans and whines rushing out of me, my cries growing sharper as his slicked fingers joined his mouth and pressed into me. His touch pushed me straight to the edge again, massaging me open as he sucked my cock until I was bucking under him, chasing my release.

He flicked my piercing with his tongue one more time, then shifted back, denying me. Again.

My eyes flew open, but before I could yell his cock replaced his fingers, sinking a few inches into me and I was lost. His mouth slanted against mine again as he sank deeper, stretching me further. And when I arched again, he stopped holding himself back.

I could hardly tell where I ended and he began, the slow but brutal pace making tears brim at the corners of my eyes. His tongue darted across my cheek again, chasing them, the muscles in his back flexing under my desperate grip for an anchor.

"Mine," he moaned out against my neck, the claim making me shudder.

His pace quickened, grinding against me with every thrust and I had to bite his shoulder to muffle my scream. A gasp tore out of him, his body clenching over mine as he felt my release between us, and he followed me straight over the edge.

The room was filled with our panted breaths, his arms shaking almost as much as my legs were. I studied him beneath half lidded eyes, the deep flush to his cheeks, the pulse of the vein in his neck. His eyes met mine a little dazed as I cupped his cheek, softening as I leaned up, kissing him gently.

He sank into it, hands brushing my hair back as he eased himself out, making both our breaths hitch. Then he was nuzzling into my neck again, heart beating steadily against my still racing one. And as my arms naturally circle his neck to keep him close, I couldn't lie to myself anymore.

My heart wasn't beating with my usual anger or fear. It was something even more dangerous that I thought I would never feel again.

Chapter 10

"Oh my *GOD*!" Jenny's squeal was loud enough to shatter glass, I swear.

"I think I'm deaf in my left ear now," I grumble, sliding my headphones back in place and chugging the rest of my coffee.

"Jackie!" She snaps, louder than my music. She was clinging to my arm now, attempting to shake me like a rag doll. "Don't you *dare* just continue on without any details!"

It had been a week since I slept with Carter. Despite my worries that he was going to become even more clingy than before, he actually settled down a bit. He met me between classes, took me to a few places to eat in the city. Spent a few more nights with me. I could tell that even though he didn't understand why I needed it, that he was trying to be discreet about it until I was ready. Which was why I had brought Jenny to the café where this all started, to try and tell her what was going on.

"Jackie!" She shook me again and I groaned, pulling my hood further over my head as the girls in the booth across from us glanced over for the third time.

"Stop making a scene and maybe I'll tell you more." She pouted, but finally freaking let go of me.

"Spill," she demanded, ignoring her own coffee to cross her arms and pretend to glare at me. I gripped my empty cup a bit tighter.

"Like I said. We've been seeing each other." I wasn't surprised she was making a big deal out of it. This was not only the first relationship I had after Andrews, but it was also one of the steadier ones I'd ever had in my life.

In high school I wasn't out. I'd stolen a few lucky kisses at parties during spin-the-bottle, but hadn't really dated until I got to college. And when I did start to date, I didn't click with anyone. It always felt awkward or forced, until Andrews.

At the time I thought I was lucky, landing an older guy. Someone mature. Patient. Then I found out about his wife and daughter, and by then I was in too far to be able to just walk away. The bastard saw to that.

"And?" Jenny pressed, interrupting the thoughts before they made me spiral. I glanced up at her. Away. Felt myself blushing as I grumbled,

"I wanna keep seeing him. It's not a big deal."

She squealed again anyway, sweeping her arms around me. I let her though, one of mine going around her waist automatically.

"He doesn't know about Andrews," I admit softly, and that gets her to settle somewhat. "I mean he knows something bad happened with an ex but not... that."

"Like you haven't told him, or that he genuinely has no idea?"

"Genuinely no idea about what happened."

I could feel myself stiffen against the idea of him finding out the truth. How I'd slept with my married advisor. How I was dragged before the board with barely any evidence that he was threatening my future. Then having it turned on me, like I'd been sleeping with him to get ahead easier than everyone else. I clear my throat, the sudden silence killing me.

"You know," Jenny says, gently drawing my gaze to hers with a hand on my cheek. "I really don't think he will react badly. I mean you called the cops on him, and he still is toting after you like a lovesick—"

"Puppy," I finish with her, a smirk pulling at my lips and she giggles.

"Its up to you," she relents, rubbing my back. "But I really think you should tell him before someone else does. You know there's still other students here from that time and..."

She trails off and I just nod my head. I knew. That's why I've been steering clear of everyone since then, just keeping a low profile and making music.

"It's also just gone so fast," I mumble, almost to myself. In pretty much a week Carter had flipped my world on its axis. Dragging me from the pit I'd buried myself in after Andrews, and pulling me back towards the light.

I've been so preoccupied with keeping my secrets and protecting my heart, I hadn't even been able to think through how I would explain myself. I doubted that doing it nonchalantly would go over well. He was a Cupid. He would want to know how involved I had been. And if he found out how brutally it ended, I didn't know what he would believe.

Not to mention the fate lines mess. He claimed to be terrified of one appearing and connecting me to someone else. Meanwhile I was terrified Andrews had broken me so badly that my fate lines had been obliterated.

"Fancy seeing the two of you here." My gaze whips up, finding Carter's smile instantly. I shut my eyes against Jenny's next squeal in my ear. She literally scrambled over top of me to throw her arms around Carter next.

"I hear things are going well," she teased instantly. Carter glanced up from her, a brow raised at me in question.

"I uh," I glanced away, feeling myself blushing again. "I mighta told her we were dating. And now she's acting like a psychopath."

When I glanced back at him his eyes were wide, but the smile on his face made the tension in me immediately ease. He untangled himself from Jenny, helping her slide into the booth seat across from me this time, before dropping beside me and slinking his arms around my waist.

"So we're officially official?"

"Saying it like that sounds stupid." He laughs, pressing a kiss to my temple anyway.

"You're sooo getting boyfriend themed Valentine's cards," Jenny says, not helping my plight. She saw me pale at least, and then actually laughed at me. "Don't tell me you forgot about Valentine's Day?"

"Shut up," I grumble, and now Carter is laughing too. He leans in even closer somehow, nuzzling beneath the barrier of my hood and speaking directly against my neck.

"I can think of a few specific ways to remind you of this holiday in particular."

"Off." He pouts but pulls back, giving me some reprieve before adding nonchalantly,

"Maybe you should both come to the party."

"Party?" I mutter, but Jenny is already glowing.

"Heavens Boys are hosting a Valentine's party?"

"Yep." Under the table Carter's free hand slides against my thigh, squeezing gently. "I insist. Come." He lowers his voice, smirking softly. "As my boyfriend."

"He accepts and we'll be there!"

"Jenny—"

"Hush you. I need to figure out what to wear. It's only a week away!"

"*You* could wear that outfit you had on at the club," Carter suggests to me. When I glance at him his smile is completely too self-satisfied. "Do whatever you did to your eyes and hair too. Let me show you off."

I was not a person to be shown off. Especially not on this campus.

"I'll text Maria. Oh Jackie, she'll be thrilled!"

"...I guess I could text Seth and see if he's willing to DJ for you guys," I offer, caving already. It was hard not to when I already felt the grin pulling at my mouth. Excitement is burning against the anxiety, and if I'm being honest with myself, it has been for a while now.

"It's a date," Carter says, hugging me around the waist tighter again. Then adds softer so only I can hear, "You have no idea how happy you've made me today."

My gut clenches with something I'm still not ready to face yet. It's too warm, too promising. But guilt is there too. I wasn't the only one excited and happy. I wasn't the only one thinking of the future, committing to this.

Jenny was right. I had to tell him. But with that beautiful look on his face right now, and held steady against his side, I couldn't. But I wouldn't drag him along either. I promised myself right there that after the party, I would face the music and tell him everything.

Chapter 11

All the excitement and confidence I had been feeling about this had thoroughly evaporated.

I thought my ears were going to bleed from the sheer number of excited shrieks at work Saturday night when Jenny told the rest of the girls I'd hooked myself a boyfriend. She and Maria had almost smothered me as they took the full hour before our shift to experiment with my hair and makeup even though I pointed out that Carter liked how it was last time.

And he didn't help things by showing up at the club both nights I was working either. Saturday he almost gave me a heart attack. I had the urge to drag him back into the staff room again, if only to button his shirt the rest of the way up. How the bouncers let him in dressed like sin and flashing his abs I have no freaking clue.

The jealousy rocketing through me every time a girl took advantage of that easy access was almost too much to bear. And the way he immediately looked up at the stage when they touched him, locking eyes with me with that sultry smirk... the bastard was getting off on making me jealous.

Sunday though he broke my stubbornness, coming in like a rock star. His usual golden boy appearance had been traded for all black leather, greased hair and eyeliner. I was staring so often that my hands kept slipping, screwing myself up. It only took one shared look with Seth for him to roll his eyes and take over for however long Carter and I locked ourselves in one of the private club rooms.

I had been on my knees before the door was even locked, feeling half possessed as I dragged him free and swallowed him down. Even after he spilled down my throat he had me bent over the low table until I was outright sobbing from the pleasure.

"Earth to Jackie." Seth smacked his hands together in front of my face. I flinched, face flooding with a blush as he yanked me out of my daydream and back to the present.

"The hell?" I yanked my earbuds out, forcing my voice to sound gruff. Then clamped my hands back down over my ears as a burst of static feedback shrieked out of the speaker behind me.

"Sorry." Seth winced, unplugging the soundboard completely. "I still don't understand how you did a party here on... this." He gestures to the dilapidated stage we're sitting on. It's somehow in even worse shape than when I was spinning for the party a few weeks ago. But they'd dragged one of those standup heaters over to it at least so Seth wouldn't have to freeze his ass off like I had.

"Gotta get creative pal."

"Is that what you told Jenny and Maria when they dolled you up?" He teased, and I narrowed my eyes at him.

"Watch it. I'll still kick your ass like this."

He held up his hands in mock surrender before going back to setting up his tech. I felt a little guilty for asking him to take a free gig but having him present—and with actual good beats—this entire experience would be more bearable and less stressful for me. I think he knew that too, since he hadn't complained about anything other than the fact his main power source was that extension cord I'd used last time.

For the millionth time I pulled out my phone, using the camera as a mirror. Maria had used the same mauve stuff, but more black than last time. Then Jenny added a touch of silver glitter for whatever 'the holiday' meant. And she simply forbade me from wearing my typical leather jacket, insisting on a more formal dress coat that she'd borrowed from her brother. All that paired with my gelled hair, I looked almost like a different person. A person I wanted to be.

"Wow." I jerk up, almost dropping my phone. Carter was standing there, looking as slack jawed as I felt. He'd gelled his hair again too, and once again I was reminded how far out of my league he was. He didn't look like he should be shuffling through a frost ridden backyard to my side.

He looked like he should be walking into a magazine shoot, with his pressed black sweater and tapered jeans.

"I don't think I'm ever going to get over seeing you with your hair like this," he said, fingers already under my chin, tilting me up for a kiss. A bolt of anxiety went through me which he immediately soothed with one more kiss to my forehead. The few people already milling around the yard weren't paying attention to us. It was okay.

"I got you something. Subtle," he added after the look I gave him. He pulled his other hand from behind his back, holding up a small corsage. It was somehow a blended rose, with red and pink petals.

"I figured traditional flowers wouldn't be your taste," he mumbles to me softly, hands already working on pinning it to my jacket. "But I am a Cupid, and as we've covered, I'm sentimental." His fingers lingered for a moment before he straightened up grinning down at whatever stupid look I probably had on my face.

"I, um, have something for you too." I turn around, yanking my bag towards me and almost send it crashing into one of Seths' speakers.

"Smooth," he mumbles, and I flip him off before ripping the zipper open, pulling out a small box.

"I know it's old tech," I explain, suddenly a little embarrassed as I hold it out towards Carter. "But I still like tangible stuff over Bluetooth if I can choose it. Call me sentimental," I add, making him chuckle softly.

He opens the box, pulling out an iPod. One of the metallic ones everyone was going nuts for in the early 2000s. Red since he's a Cupid. God I'm dramatic.

"It has fifty songs already saved. Some old ones I think you'd like. Some new ones I know you like. Some of mine that I finally finished." I swallow, my throat suddenly dry with nerves. "I know its stupid considering we have Spotify and all that crap now but I—"

"It's not stupid." He cuts me off with ease, dropping to his knees in front of me and hugging me tight to his chest. "I love it," he murmurs, voice muffled against my chest. "I love—"

"Y-you're gonna break the corsage or something," I blurt out. My heart beats against my ribcage, like a wild animal trying to break free. Was he really about to say what I thought he was going to say?

Instead of being angry when he eases back, he just smiles up at me again. So soft. So sure.

"...I'm glad you love it." I finally manage words, quietly. Lean forward and press a kiss to his own forehead.

"And I'm glad your sappy exchange is finally finished, because I'm about to start blasting," Seth cuts in, snickering slightly when my cheeks go up in flames.

I let Carter tug me to my feet, leaving the stage as Seth turns the volume up, music rolling through the open air. A chorus of shouts and whoops go up, students flooding out of the frat house and into the yard. I see Jenny, covered head to toe in pink with angel wings on her back. I want to go over to her, but I know she'll snap at me for running away from Carter. And his grip on me just tightened anyway.

"We don't have to stay out here long," he says, low in my ear. "I know you don't like crowds much."

My chest ached. He learned what he could about me and always took it into consideration, without me needing to say a word. I leaned into his side a little more, shaking my head.

"I know you love this kind of stuff. I'm good." That million-watt smile again.

"Then let me go get you a drink. We'll dance some. I'll introduce you to some of the guys, and we'll go from there. Okay?" I was a little apprehensive of meeting other students, unsure if I'd still be recognized, but forced a smile on my face and nodded. I couldn't keep hiding forever.

"I'll wait over there." I point to one of the heaters by the stairs. Farthest from the stage, and the crowd in the yard. Starting slowly.

Carter left me with a wink, and I shoved my hands in my pockets, trudging over. I released a shaky breath as I leaned back against the porch railing, watching my breath cloud in front of me before the heater made it disappear. A few undergrads stumbled down the stairs, one saluting in my direction which was weird but... not negative. I could do this.

At least that's what I thought until a familiar voice curled into my ears, making a cold wash of fear flood my nervous system.

"It's been a while, Jackson."

Chapter 12

Andrews took a sip of his beer, eyes locked on me where I stood frozen.

It didn't take a genius to figure out he was wasted already, the drink in his hand definitely not his first as he sagged against the railing over me. That finally got me to lurch back, my hands instantly balling to fists at my sides.

"Aren't you a little old for frat parties?" I growled out. Forget that, he wasn't even supposed to be on campus. He'd been barred by the board, plus my restraining order. Still, he barked out a laugh anyway, his eyes gleaming with twisted delight as they travelled the length of me.

"Aren't you a little old for your new boy toy?" He rasped back, and all the anger I felt shifted to fear again. His grin was wicked as he nodded his head, straightening up.

"That's right. I know all about you and that little undergrad you've been fucking." He paused, head tilting for a second before laughing again. "Or would it be him fucking you? Probably. You were always more than willing to bend over."

"Shut up." It came out with far less venom than I wanted it to. "Just shut up and get the fuck out of here."

"Jackson?" A fresh bolt of fear went through me as Carter's voice sounded behind me. Low, and confused. Not like himself at all. I was too afraid to look at him. Too afraid to move.

"Jackson," Andrews echoed again, sounding outright pissed. "Not Jackie? You're letting this little shit have the same privileges I did?"

I winced, my gaze dropping to the ground, blurring as panic clouded my brain. There was already a crowd gathering, the whispers starting again. I started shaking as I heard someone gasp out a 'that Jackson' and fought the urge to bolt. This couldn't be happening again.

"Jackie?" Jenny's voice behind me, her hand cupping my cheek and forcing my head up. Her gaze flicking to the porch, eyes widening, then glaring.

"What the hell are you doing here?" She snaps, tightening her hold on me protectively.

"Collecting a debt," Andrews sneered down at her. "This doesn't involve you Jennifer."

"Jackie lets go. Carter can you call campus security?"

Carter.

My gaze whips around to find him. His face was eerily blank, doe eyes slowly shifting between Andrews and where I stood frozen.

"Carter," Andrews drawled out, and I winced like he'd actually hit me. "So that's your name. I didn't catch it over the past few weeks I've been watching you two."

"You've been stalking Jackson?" Carter asked slowly, the drinks in his hands spilling slightly.

"That little shit ruined my life," Andrews barked out. "Ended my career, my marriage—"

Carter was a blur past us, cutting Andrews off with a right hook to the jaw. My own jaw dropped as he crashed down onto the porch, but Carter wasn't done. He pounced on him, caging him beneath him and started wailing on him. Blood was spraying against the porch making one of the girls scream and I finally broke out of my paralyzed state.

"Fuck!" I scrambled up the stairs, catching Carters arm mid-swing. "Help me!" I snapped at two of his frat brothers. They dropped their beers, grabbing Carter by the shoulders and helped me heave him back.

I didn't stop dragging him until my back was braced against the side of the house, arms around Carter's torso to keep him pinned against me. Andrews was half curled on his side, one hand covering his brutalized face. I couldn't even tell if he was conscious or not.

"Carter?" I whispered, terrified of how hard he was shaking in my arms.

Seth had blasted the music louder to draw people away from the scene, but was already off the stage helping a few of Heavens Boys haul Andrews to his feet and back through the house. Jenny was on her phone at the bottom of the steps, and from the shaking in her voice I could tell it was with the cops.

My stomach lurched into my chest as that realization. Not again. I couldn't do this again. I couldn't let Carter get in trouble because of this.

"That was the guy saved in your phone as A, right?" Carters voice was rougher than normal, and instinctively my grip on him tightened.

"Yes."

His hands rose to cover mine on his chest, squeezing tight enough for my fingers to crack.

"He had a fate line reaching for you. A black one." I froze again, the sounds of everything around us fading to background noise. Carter finally tilted his head back to look at me, his eyes still wild. "I will never let him near you again. I promise."

I didn't even realize I was crying until his hand left mine, his thumb brushing the tears away. There was no fight left in me as he sat up on his knees, twisting to scoop me in his arms and carry me inside. Someone mentioned something about the police, but he ignored them, taking me straight up the stairs and to his room.

"Carter," I found my voice, finally protesting as he kicked the door shut behind us. "I'm going to have to talk to them. And Jenny is still—"

"You didn't do anything wrong," he cut me off, setting me on the edge of the bed. "They can wait until tomorrow. You need to calm down, and rest."

"But I did!" I snapped, jerking away from his as he reached for me. His eyes shuttered, annoyance flaring off him, but he paused.

"What Andrews said was true," I whispered, my voice shaking. "I was sleeping with him for most of my undergrad. His wife found out. Our relationship got him fired and—"

"I know." Carter grabbed me by the chin, forcing me to look at him. "I felt like an asshole looking into your history, but I knew something was wrong. And I'm going to say it as many times as I have to before you finally believe it." He knelt in front of me again, both hands cupping my face now.

"You didn't do anything wrong."

I didn't know how badly I needed to hear those words. My arms hooked around his neck, and he came down to me, tucking me into his chest as I finally let everything to the surface. And for the first time in three years, the sense of drowning was finally relieved.

Chapter 13

Carter was lucky, the police had said. Since Andrews had already violated two legal orders, Carters actions were considered an act of self-defense.

He'd put him in the hospital. Broken nose, stitches, a concussion. I knew that level of violence should concern me, but I couldn't find it in myself to care. Carter blandly expressed his sympathies, but I could tell he didn't care either. Jenny had flat out said Andrews deserved it, making the interviewing cop sigh.

They had agreed to the request for me to give my statement in the morning. With my history of panic attacks and depression since the original case, they probably didn't want to push me too hard.

Kept everything basic too, which I appreciated. It was done a hell of a lot faster than the first time.

And then it was time for the hard part. Once the cops had gone, Jenny sat by my side, holding my hand as I explained everything to Carter. How at first my relationship with Andrews had been genuine, but when I found out he had a family I wanted to break it off and then it became something else entirely.

He claimed to have my future in his hands, threatened to destroy it all and get me kicked out of school. So, for two years I endured more of it, until his wife caught us. The civil case. Being put on the stand and having to confirm and deny what aspects of our relationship were consensual or forced and when it changed.

The only evidence I had was the notes from my therapist. I hadn't told her who Andrews was, but for a year I'd seen her once a week. While we talked about my abusive relationship she taught me coping mechanisms while I searched for a safe way out. It was humiliating, but after her testimony the jury sided in my favor.

Carter listened patiently through it, his hand rubbing slow circles on my lower back. I could tell he was livid, but reigned it in, once again telling me that I hadn't done anything wrong. I really hoped I started feeling that way soon.

At that point Jenny excused herself, kissing me on the temple before she left. Gave Carter a matching one, and then let us be so we could talk.

His knuckles were bruised to hell and back from hitting Andrews so hard, and I couldn't help the flash of guilt through me. He caught my gaze on them, shaking his head.

"I have some questions now, if that's alright?" I nodded my head, mentally bracing myself. "What are you doing after you graduate?"

I stared at my lap. The plan had always been to get my master's in music production, and drag my way out to LA. I hadn't thought of any other options besides that. But Carter still had a year of his undergrad and would be halfway across the country.

"Honestly... I don't know now," I admitted, hands balling to fists in my lap. "I only ever thought of it one way."

Carter nodded his head, then flopped back down on the mattress beside me. A few minutes of silence stretched out as we both thought.

"Can I make a selfish request?" He finally asked, voice so soft I barely heard it.

I turned to look down at him, brow arching as his nervous gaze stayed locked on the ceiling.

"Whatever you decide to do," he says, swallowing hard. "Would you be okay with including me in it?"

"Are you an idiot?" His gaze shot to mine, visibly anxious until I leaned over him, pressing a kiss to his mouth.

I poured everything I hadn't said into it, every thought, every hope. Only pulled back far enough to be able to mumble, "I'm not breaking up with you just because I'm graduating, Cupid."

His arms latched around my waist, keeping me there, kissing me again. Hungry. The tension in both our bodies from the past twelve hours needing a place to go.

He nipped my lower lip as he dragged me on top of him, hands sliding under the back of my shirt to trace my bare skin.

"I just," his mouth covered mine again before I could finish and I sighed, sliding my hand around his throat. He lets out a low sound when I squeezed, but relented.

"I just need to figure out logistics," I panted out against his mouth. "That's all."

"My mind is on very different logistics," he murmured, and I grinned, my legs on either side of him gripping tighter. His hands smoothed over my ass, yanking me up a few inches higher on his waist.

"You're insufferable," I groaned out and he chuckled, knowing he'd won.

Our clothes hit the floor slowly, hands roaming over every inch of each other with reverence. His breath hitched when I finally slid a hand down, stroking him leisurely.

"Jackson—"

"Give me the lube," I whisper. Then smirked down at the shocked look on his face, tilting my head. "Unless you want me to stop?"

His hand scrambled across his nightstand, knocking a few items onto the floor as he yanked the drawer open. I chuckled as I wet one of my hands, returning it to his length and slicking him from root to tip. A whip of satisfaction coursed through me when he immediately moaned, bucking up into my palm.

I stopped making him wait, shedding the rest of my clothes and angling my body to take him in. His hands had a vicelike grip on my waist as I sank onto him, my eyes falling shut against the stretch. And only after a small nod from me did he start to move.

His head arched back as I met each of his thrusts, his ragged breaths serving as encouragement. I drank in the way his muscles tensed every time I was seated fully, the way his gasps were beginning to match the roll of my hips.

"Harder," I breathed out, eyes half lidded as I lowered over him. My mouth latched to his bared throat a half second before his thrusts shifted from languid to rough and I moaned into his skin. He snapped at the sound, rolling me onto my back and hooking my legs around his waist.

His hand closed around my cock as he chased his release, smothering my cries with his mouth. He came first, pinning me with his full weight. His hand on my length tightening.

"Say you're mine, Jackson."

"I'm yours."

There was no reason to fight it anymore. And as he stroked me to the edge of bliss I dragged his mouth down to mine again, claiming him as he claimed me.

Chapter 14

Nine months later

The funny thing about New England was the seasons did whatever the hell they wanted. By some miracle graduation came and went, and I walked for the second and last time. Carter's friends ceremony was separate from mine, so he didn't have to miss anyone's which was nice. Jenny came as his plus one, screaming loud enough for me to pick them out of the crowd.

And to his absolute delight he got to meet my mother. By the time I got off stage she was cradling a bundle of pink roses I think were originally meant for me, but I was happy to let her keep them.

Carter had been in the hot seat for once with all the questions and curiosities, but of course he handled the pressure perfectly. So perfectly in fact, it was his arm my mother reached for as we left the restaurant, tipsy and giggling with Jenny. It soothed something in me, seeing her so happy. After all the drama the past few years I was worried I would just continue to disappoint her. I could stop worrying about that now.

The summer had been hard, going home to Maine for a few weeks. Carter had also taken a trip home to Chicago, promising to bring his parents out when he returned. His dad was apparently a retired Cupid, his mother a normal person like me. I was scared shitless meeting them the first time, but I didn't have to be. His mother had smacked both him and his father on the back of the head as soon as they mentioned my lack of fate lines, taking me by the arm to go get drinks without those 'buffoons' she called them. I couldn't help but laugh.

As for LA... I backed it up a year. My work in Providence landed me a six-month paid internship in New York City which I was happy to take. I paid my share in rent for the apartment the two other interns and I shared, but caught a train back to Rhode Island during the week to stay with Carter when I could.

He'd left the frat house, and Jenny was more than happy to let him rent a room in the apartment she and Maria shared. And honestly, after years of living in solo dorms, renting with friends was actually pretty damn nice. Though I'm pretty sure she and Maria were secretly dating, but I didn't push for answers.

As for Seth, he went to LA. Apparently he had literally been hanging out, waiting till I graduated to go with him and keep being his partner. I told him he was an idiot for keeping that a secret, but with the way things turned out, we both decided it was for the best. Though I did shove him on the plane with the promise to talk me up, help me get my foot in the door when Carter and I moved out there next year.

Which we were already planning even though it was only his Thanksgiving break.

"I think your mom and my mom are scheming."

"Hmm?" I slid my headphones off an ear, glancing up from my new laptop. Carter pointed behind me to the high table where our mothers were huddled, sipping on iced lattes and thumbing through the stack of listings the realtor had given us.

When we told them we wanted to come out and look at a few houses Seth said we might like, they insisted on coming with.

And his parents were awesome about it, even willing to cover the down payment and co-sign the lease so we wouldn't have to wait.

"I swear to god they're going to try and convince us to get the green one."

"Not happening," I murmur, turning the volume down on the track I'm working and lean back, stretching my arms over my head. As expected he takes the opening, sweeping in and pressing a kiss to my cheek.

"It had its charm."

"You didn't like it either."

"True."

"I have a feeling I'm going to like the blue one. With the terrace." I arched a brow, not remembering that one.

"Why?" I asked, already mentally preparing for whatever outlandish idea he had. His sneaky looking grin just added fuel to that fire, so I slid my elbow back into his ribs gently. "Spill."

"Because it's kind of been in my family for roughly three centuries." I outwardly gaped at him and he laughed.

"Then why the hell have we been looking at houses to buy!? In this neighborhood? Market?"

He laughed heartily as I swat at him and slid off my stool. Smoothly, he wrapped an arm around my waist as his free hand intercepted the laptop, sliding it into my saddlebag hanging off the back of my chair. Then cupped my chin in that way that always got him what he wanted.

"I just didn't want you to feel backed into a corner with it. I wanted you to know you had options." Fuck me, he was too good for me. And I was never freaking let him go. His smile widened as I tried to mask how touched I was with a huff, then glanced over my head towards our mothers.

"Mom. Jackson has decided he wants to look at the South Bay house."

I ignored the flurry of excitement behind me, sliding my bag onto my shoulder instead. Carter eased my headphones fully off to rest around my neck, pulling me impossibly closer.

"Is now a good time to mention it has a finished basement which would make an excellent studio space?"

"Keep talking like that and I won't even have to see it to want it," I murmur and he laughs.

His hand slides off my waist to push the door open for our mothers to spill out towards the car. His mother was swiping through photos on her phone, of what I'm assuming was the house since mine was plastered to her side. He catches my hand though as I head after them, holding me back for a half second.

"Will you say it for me?" His eyes were damn near glittering in the sunlight, his tone dipping to something sultrier. I told myself the warmth in my cheeks was from the California sun.

"Here? On a crummy sidewalk?" I force the annoyance in my voice, fingers fiddling with the chord on my headphones. He catches them again, rolling his thumb over the silver band adorning mine. My eyes instantly latch onto his matching one.

"I want to hear it everywhere. Every day," he says cupping my cheek again. "Especially here, on a crummy sidewalk before I give you a tour of our future home."

His lips close over mine. Soft and slow. Enough time to let me both process what he just said, and fluster me from the public display.

"Fine," I grumble, and he gives me that million-watt, happy golden retriever puppy smile that I adore. I quickly press my lips to his again, then bring my mouth to his ear.

"I love you. Now can we go to the car before our mothers skip house hunting and jump straight to wedding planning?"

His fingers are laced tightly through mine again, one of my songs playing as quiet background music as we drive. As the buildings give way to an ocean view, I knew I'd never need a fate line to know I was exactly where I was meant to be.

Authors Note

I have been a long-time fan of BL stories and shows, and hope I did the genre justice with my first attempt at creating one. The first reason why I decided to venture here is because in romances I often can't relate much to the girls archetypes. Like Jackie, I'm a tsundere. Loudly apprehensive and avoid getting my heart involved. I bury myself deep because underneath the hard shell, I loathe to admit that my husband is right and I'm a softie.

The second reason I wrote this is just as simple: we need more LGBTQ+ books. From as many voices and perspectives as possible. While I'm not a boy like my characters, I do identify as pansexual and represent that through Carter's character. When it comes down to it, at the end of the day we ALL deserve to be yearned for, supported, and loved as we are.

I want to close out with a special thanks to the friends who made the time to read and give feedback on this story in the short time frame my ADHD allowed. And as always, my deepest thanks and gratitude to my readers. With grace, love, and a fair amount of chaos,   *Nightshade*